Becoming Dragon

Dragon Point

Eve Langlais

New York Times Bestseller

Copyright © July 2016, Eve Langlais
Cover Art by Yocla Designs © July 2016
Edited by Devin Govaere
2nd Edit by Amanda Pederick
3rd Edit by Chelle Olson
Produced in Canada

Published by Eve Langlais
1606 Main Street, PO Box 151
Stittsville, Ontario, Canada, K2S1A3
http://www.EveLanglais.com

ISBN-13: 978-1537526034
ISBN-10: 1537526030

ALL RIGHTS RESERVED

Chapter One

"What the fuck did you do to me?" *I'm a monster.* There was no other word for what he'd become. The mirror didn't lie.

"You are a soldier for the future. A shining example of what anyone can become." The man who'd done this to him didn't even have the courtesy to look ashamed. He justified his vile act.

Because he wants us to kill him.

"Why would anyone choose to become thisss?" The words emerged with a sibilant hiss, his tongue having split to become more serpent's than man's. He lifted his fingers and noted their change, the claws at the tips, the coarse and scaly skin. No part of him remained untouched. He didn't dare take a peek inside his pants.

Here lizard, lizard. He ignored the other voice.

"Who wouldn't choose to be stronger and faster? You should thank me for the improvement. Especially since it didn't cost you a thing." His uncle held the same cold stare he always did, but his lips curved, hinting at a smirk. A smirk Brandon wanted to smash.

To think he'd been excited when his rich relative came for a visit months ago. *Want to come work for me?* How he wished instead he'd done as his mother recommended when she spotted Uncle Theo stepping out of his luxury car. *"Get the shotgun and shoot that varmint."* But Brandon chose to follow the financial lure promised by his uncle's swanky clothes and expensive wheels.

"You are deluded if you think I'll thank you for making me a frrr-eak." Brandon found it hard to control the lisp. He no longer truly had lips, and his tongue wasn't the one he'd been born with—the one he used to kiss the girls so they'd drop their panties for kisses elsewhere.

They might not want a kiss now. He kept his lips clamped, lest he hiss. Not for the first time, he wished things had never changed.

I wish I hadn't changed.

Nothing about him was how it used to be, except for his eyes. Those bright brown orbs appeared so out of place within his monstrous new visage. He couldn't stop staring at the face in the mirror. The scaly skin, the thick ridges across his cheeks, the alien nature of his features. Shocking. *I no longer look human.* Then again, he had never been quite human, not even at birth.

"Congrats, it's an alligator," the midwife, also known as his Aunt Darlene, had announced after she'd helped birth his, according to his mother, "Fat head"—spoken with the utmost affection and also quite true. All the Mercer boys had big noggins. A good thing, too, since they got smacked around a lot—by each other, the joys of a large family. As for Ma, why give them a smack when she only had to point that evil eye in their direction for them to behave, and by *behave* he should note that bar was perhaps a little lower than the usual, the one other, more civilized folk adhered to.

Brandon was a gator shifter, descended from a long line of swamp gators. Most of them miscreants. More than a few in jail or just out of. And Brandon had fit right in. At least, he used to. Now with his mutant shape, he didn't know who he was anymore. *What am I?*

Better. The cold thought wasn't his own, so he ignored it.

"Change me back," Brandon demanded. He couldn't live like this.

"No." A flat, one-syllable reply that ignited his anger.

He whirled around to confront his uncle, the smarmy bastard in his custom-fitted suit and his coiffed hair. Fucking pansy. He even wore some girly fucking scent, but it didn't camouflage the smell of asshole.

A mottled green fist shot out as he grabbed Uncle Theo by the lapels and lifted him. He brought his face close and growled, "Fix me." Brandon punctuated the demand with a shake—which he considered pretty restrained, given his first impulse was to rip the bastard to shreds.

Do it. Eat the flesh of our enemy. Crunch.

No. He wasn't that kind of monster.

Yet.

Not an ounce of fear entered Theo's gaze. His expression remained flat. "Have you forgotten the terms of our bargain?"

Of course, he hadn't. It had all started a week after his sister had gone missing, and it turned out Theo had her. Brandon remembered the conversation.

"You let us run a few experiments, and your little sister goes free."

"Will these tests hurt?"

"Would I hurt family?"

Brandon should have known better than to trust the wide smile with the white, capped teeth.

Turned out, Uncle Theo would and *could* hurt family. In his quest for power, he didn't mind using his nieces and nephews to further his agenda, which, on the surface, was to improve the plight of shifters and make breakthroughs in the field of experimental treatments. In truth, Theo wanted to make hybrid shifters, soldier shifters that he could sell to the highest bidders. But his madness didn't stop there. He even had plans to change humans, who could pay the price, too.

"I remember our bargain, but I didn't agree to this." Brandon swept a hand across his body, more lizard on two legs than man. The wings at his back fluttered with his agitation.

Wings. Fucking wings. Birds flew, not six-foot-plus men—unless someone tossed them across a room in a barroom brawl.

"Stop your whining. It's too late to go back now. The changes cannot be reversed. Your DNA has been spliced, fused into something new. This is who you are now. Get used to it."

Rage filled Brandon and needed an outlet. He shook his uncle. "I will not get used to it. You made me into a monster."

"And I'll make your sister one, too, if you don't release me," shouted his uncle, finally losing his cool.

Hurt Sue-Ellen? The threat froze Brandon. He

dropped his uncle, even if inside he seethed, a dark wrath that demanded justice.

Needsss blood. The cold presence of his beast spoke to him very clearly, stronger now in this form. Not necessarily a good thing, given his animal side saw things in more basic—AKA, violent—terms. His gator wasn't one to cater to affection.

"Don't you dare hurt my sister."

Theo smoothed the lapel of his jacket. "Behave, and she never has to see the inside of a lab. I've got other plans for her."

"If you dare lay a hand or anything else on her…"

"Why would I do that? She's family. And I still need her." His uncle smiled, and while he might have Mercer blood running through his veins, it was Lupine, not gator. His uncle was a wolf, the big bad wolf. "There's a reason I'm considered the smart one in the family. I don't compromise my assets, but I also won't tolerate disobedience. You will obey me."

"Suck my dick." At least Brandon hoped he still had one. He'd yet to take a peek.

"We have other plans for your sperm, dear nephew. Another stage of our plans will involve impregnating women with your modified spermatozoids. We want to see if your new genes transfer to your progeny."

"You're sick."

"I am a man who is looking forward to the future. A future we shall own. ·It is time our kind stopped hiding in the shadows. It is time we took our spots at the heads of governments. Lycans and other shapeshifters are the predators of this world. We were meant to rule." Theo's very words were treason against all shifters.

"You're a madman."

"I prefer the term, *visionary*. Now, if you'll excuse me, I do have other business to attend to."

"What about me? What happens now?" Going home was out of the question. His family would lose their shit if they saw him.

"What happens is you will stay under observation. While the genetic splice appears to be a success, it remains to be seen whether your mind can handle it. "

"What do you mean, whether my mind can handle it?"

"We've had issues with other subjects. Minor setbacks. The humans we've modified all seem to turn into mindless animals. They're weak and can't handle the beast."

"What about the shifters? What happens to them?"

"That depends on you, and your beast. But just in case you lose that battle, we have to take precautions."

His uncle turned to a table and opened the box sitting on it. Brandon didn't react at all when his uncle pivoted to face him holding a hinged ring of metal.

Thisss isn't good, his cold side advised. *Should bite him.*

He would most certainly not bite—unless backed into a corner. A corner that was pretty fucking close, given that his uncle held up the ring and said, "Put it on."

"No." Like hell would he collar himself. A collar would make a slave of him. It would take away all of his control. It wasn't just Braveheart who'd screamed freedom. Every man's and beast's instinct was to never let anyone fetter them.

"You will put this on, or I will have my people put it on you. Your choice."

"Go ahead and try. I'll die first."

"Die? Oh no, not after the trouble I've gone through to remake you. But at the same time, while I won't let you expire, I see no reason to tell my staff to be gentle. The doctors are curious to see if your healing ability has increased at all."

"Don't you have any conscience at all about doing this? Were you not hugged as a child? Were you that freakazoid kid who pulled the legs off spiders?"

"Actually, it was frog legs, and they were quite delicious, especially when Grand-Mère battered and deep fried them. And to answer your question, my conscience is clear. I act for the greater good of my kind."

"This isn't good for us."

"It is for me, as it means power and money."

The man was a raving lunatic. Brandon couldn't let him go through with his plan. He would put all of them in jeopardy. "I won't let you do this!" Brandon dove at Theo and managed to clasp the metal ring. He fully intended to rip it from his uncle's grip and snap it around Theo's neck.

It took only one name to drop him to his knees. "Sue-Ellen."

It sucked the fight from him. His fingers went limp, and his arms fell back to his sides as he bowed his head in submission.

No. Sacrifice the youngling. Do not do thisss. Bite

him. Fight.

The list of violent suggestions continued, but he wouldn't give in to the seeping coldness within. *I am not a monster.*

His knees hit the floor.

No. The rage in his head hissed and thrashed, but while he might appear a beast on the outside, Brandon was still a man. A man who would do anything for his little sister.

It proved hard not to flinch when the metal curved around his neck, a harsh reminder of what he was now.

Nothing. *I am no one.*

And over the next weeks, he quickly learned to obey commands, even the heinous ones, the electrical shocks they poured through his body a harsh punishment. Disobeying wasn't an option.

So he did things.

Horrible things.

He hated himself, but he hated his uncle even more, which was why, when the day of reckoning finally arrived, and Brandon broke the chains of bondage that held him, he set off after Theo, and his sister.

The dark within demanded vengeance—and dinner. *Crunch.*

Chapter Two

"Hairy, three-balled, humping son of a Sasquatch, what the fuck is that idiot doing?" her twin sister, Adrianne, yelled.

Given this happened quite often—the yelling, not the Bigfoots with a third testis—Aimi didn't pay much attention. Her hot-headed other half spent much of her time yelling at something. Or someone. What you needed to fear was the silence.

"The gods-damned apocalypse is here. Quick, Aimi, grab the keys for the Suburban. We need to go into town and hit the bulk store to stock up. Shit is going to get ugly. Really fucking ugly."

"It will get even uglier if you keep cussing like that. Or have you so soon forgotten what Aunt Yolanda did last time she heard you acting unladylike."

Soap wasn't considered strong enough for a filthy mouth. They got to gargle castor oil.

Shudder.

"I bet even Aunt Yolanda drops an f-bomb when she hears about the moron who just told the whole world shifters are real."

"Are you watching the Bigfoot-hunting dudes again?"

"No. This is on CNN."

"What?" The mention of the news channel caught Aimi's attention. She moved toward her sister and found her gaze riveted to the television screen. While the image proved grainy, she could see some kind of jouncing camera recording a crazy scene. Animals fighting each other; gators and bears and wolves and even some humans with guns. A chaotic mess that even had a moose charging through. The ticker bar and voice-over were even more strange.

"This is some of the video footage we received anonymously just moments before reporters arrived at the private medical compound situated only a few miles from the Everglades. The Bittech Institute is supposedly a medical research facility, but preliminary reports are stating it was more than that. It was run by…shapeshifters?" The on-screen anchor couldn't help a disbelieving lilt. "Seriously?" The news anchor shook her blonde, helmet-stiff-gelled head, but a true pro, she went on. "According to Theodore Parker, the CEO of Bittech, shapeshifters have been walking among us for thousands of years, mostly undetected."

"Because humans are twat-waffles who never look further than their own shortcomings." Her sister threw a handful of popcorn at the screen, leaving a grease mark on the glass and adding another pile of crumbs to the floor. They'd tried having pets as children to eat the foodstuffs they dropped. However, all of them had run away. Strange how that happened.

"Why must you be such a slob?"

"Don't be such a clean freak. I'm doing my part to stimulate the economy by providing employment for housecleaners. It's people like you, who clean up after themselves, that put people out of work. Good job hating your fellow citizens."

"Is this where I'm supposed to thank you for being a slob?"

"Just thinking of the little people," said quite seriously by her sister, the mentality of a spoiled princess in a punk-rocker body. The chain looping from her nose to her ear was a nice touch.

But the piercings and rainbow pixie hair didn't change one fact. "You are the epitome of a rich bitch, you know that, right?"

Her sister grinned, her perfect smile gleaming. "Why, thank you. I try my best. I did, after all, learn from the master." Also known as Zahra, their mother. "Enough of my greatness. We have something only slightly more important to discuss. The end of the world."

"Why the end? Did someone launch a bomb? Did they find a meteor? Is the core of the Earth overheating and about to blow us up?" Aimi might have a slight addiction to apocalypse-type movies.

"None of the above. I'm talking about the fact that shifters are about to go to war with mankind."

"We don't know that will happen."

Her sister aimed the remote and rewound the news footage and replayed the animals running wild and, in at least one case, attacking a human.

Okay, so there was a possibility that the humans might get a little trigger-happy. Oh, who was she kidding. Humans would freak and go on a werewolf hunt.

I should make a quick call to my broker and buy some silver stocks. She should also invest in garlic. For some reason, when people got superstitious, they fell back to the basics.

"You're thinking of making money, aren't you?" her sister accused.

"Aren't you?"

"Of course." Her sister rolled her eyes. "I took care of your stuff, too. I predict the price of silver is going to shoot through the roof."

Nothing like increasing her net worth to make her feel warm and fuzzy inside.

"So, do you want to come with me on a run to the store for necessities?"

"You do realize Mother and our aunts probably already have storerooms of supplies just in case the apocalypse does come."

"Hoarding bitches," coughed her sister.

"Says the girl who sneaks all the boxes of Twinkies out of the kitchen as soon as the groceries are delivered each week."

"I do what I must to save you. Your ass can thank me later when it doesn't fall out of your bikini bottom. Now, come on, let's go paint the town."

Why not? Aimi could use a break from being in the house and listening to her mother's constant harping: "When are you going to find a mate? Would you stop harassing your cousins? Getting arrested for drunk and disorderly isn't how we stay low-key."

As if it were Aimi's and her cousins' fault the cop who pulled them over didn't have a sense of humor.

"I'll go, but I'm driving," she announced.

"You drove last time," Adi said with a pout.

"Because I'm the one who still has a license. Or have you forgotten that pesky thing called the law?"

"Those human things shouldn't apply to us."

"And yet, they do, and you know what Mother said she'd do if you got arrested again." Force her sister to dye her hair back to her normal color, lose the nose piercing, and start wearing proper dresses with pantyhose and fat-heeled pumps.

The shudder in her sister proved most pronounced. "Mother is evil."

"She is, which is why I'm driving."

"Fine." Her sister bounded off the couch. "I call shotgun."

"Who else is coming?"

Adi shrugged. "I don't know, but chances are, Deka and Babette will want to come, too."

They hadn't even managed two steps when the dreaded voice stopped them. "And where do you think you're going?" Mother asked as she swept into the family room of their mansion. Although "family room" seemed a misnomer. It implied an intimate place for a few to gather.

In Aimi's world, a family room was more like a grand ballroom with a huge open space, three-stories tall, ringed in balconies, and, hanging in a few places, swings, suspended by chains and wrapped in silk flowers. No nets below, she might add. Nets were for the clumsy who shouldn't procreate, according to her Aunt Yolanda.

On the main floor sat a myriad of game tables—billiards, foosball, air hockey, arcades, and more—along with several couches and a few televisions, all of them hooked to the most recent game systems.

This was where the kids hung out, and

according to their mother and aunts, even at the ripe age of twenty-seven, Aimi and Adrianne were still kids.

Single ones, who had yet to move out because, in her world, only married girls got to move out to start their family line.

The whole bra-burning thing had kind of passed them by on account the women already ruled in the family—for some reason, they tended to birth way more girls than boys. Because of this, they abided by some self-imposed, quirky rules. The big one being: have babies, but not just any babies, family-approved ones.

"We were just going to go out and maybe hit a restaurant for dinner and then a movie." Adi never had learned to lie very well.

Their mother's gaze narrowed, the violet of her eyes dark, the regard suspicious. "This sudden desire to hang with humans wouldn't have anything to do with the news coming out of Florida, would it?"

"News? What news?" Adi stated, even as the report on the television at her back flipped to yet more footage of animals running wild.

"Your ability to play stupid is astounding."

"Not really, I'm pretty good at acting oblivious and ignoring things, too."

The jests did not lighten their mother's expression at all.

"I take it you heard what's happening?" Aimi asked, trying to divert attention from her twin.

"Of course, I heard. You know how closely Vanna and Valda monitor the news stations and the internet for out-of-the-ordinary tidbits. We've been expecting this for a while now. However, it did happen a tad sooner than predicted. Something must have forced the SHC"—short for the Shifter High Council—"to move up their timeline."

The reply took Aimi by surprise. "You knew the Cryptozoids would do this?" Cryptozoids being a fancy name for creatures that weren't human and believed to not exist.

"There is little we don't know. But we did have advance warning from the SHC. Mainly from that mongrel, Parker. A few years back, Parker met with several of the Sept heads"—the Septs being the dragon version of a pack, divided by color and varying in power depending on their strength and size—"and made some valid points about revealing the existence of shifters and other species. He argued the world had changed too much for the Cryptozoids to remain hidden. It was just a matter of time before the shifter secret came out. Even we are not safe, despite the measures we've taken to keep our existence secret." Those that discovered what they were didn't live long, and yet the trail of deaths couldn't be traced back to them because no one ever found the bodies.

Only amateurs leave evidence behind.

"You're being rather blasé about the situation. Aren't you worried at all?" Aimi asked.

"Worried about what? The shifters may do as they please."

"So does this mean we're coming out of the castle, too?" Adi asked.

"Not exactly. After Parker had revealed his plans to us, we engaged in many discussions with the other Sept leaders. It was decided that should the revelation come to pass, we would let the lower-born weather the initial shock."

"By 'weather,' you mean let the humans go crazy and hunt the shifters. Are you planning to hand them pitchforks, too, and point them in the right direction?" Adi, the voice of pessimism and anarchy.

"We can't be sure that will happen. We live in an age where differences are now protected by laws." And yet, even Aimi didn't entirely believe there would be peace. She had watched her fair share of paranormal shows and movies. It seemed, without fail, the inhuman had to die.

Then again, humans made the movies. What if the Cryptos did? History was shaped by the winners. Imagine a world where they didn't have to hide, and those that crossed them succumbed to the old ways, the recipes to eradicate them contained in a grimoire kept locked away.

"You are naïve if you think this will go over well. The humans fear what they don't understand." Her mother shook her head. "Mark my words, we will see blood running in the streets. Mayhem and lawlessness will flourish. Many will die."

"And you're just going to sit back and allow it?"

"What else would you have us do?"

Aimi lifted her hands and shrugged. "Something. Anything."

"For centuries, kings and queens have let their pawns fight the battles."

"You're talking about letting humans and shifters go to war."

"The humans are already at war with each other. It's all over the news. Every day, a new shooting and bombing. The governments will welcome a chance for reprieve, and what better way to draw nations together than to fight a common enemy?"

Sometimes, her mother's cold, calculated nature stunned. Aimi wasn't averse to doing what had to be done, but even she drew the line somewhere. "If it comes to war, millions will die."

"And if that happens, then the earth might have a chance to recover from humanity's excesses."

"Did you seriously just solve pollution by countenancing the eradication of a good portion of the population?"

"The simple elegance of it is stunning, don't you think? Once the chaos has died down, and both sides are tired of the fighting, we shall step into leadership roles. If you ask me, this is great news for our kind."

"Add in an evil laugh, and you'll sound like a dictator." Aimi couldn't help but shake her head at her mother's bloodthirsty ambition.

"Dictators get the job done. Have you not studied our history at all? Have some pride in your roots."

"Is that why you're here? To remind us that we're snotty princesses in hiding?"

"Actually, I need you and your sister bathed and changed into something nice. Eugenia and her son are coming for a visit."

"Would that be the son who always smells like garlic?" He also sported greasy hair, lacked a few inches in height, and might have been inbred, given that his intelligence was lower than most household pets.

"He is a lovely young man. A *single* young man."

"Since when? Wasn't he married to what's-her-face?" Adi snapped her fingers. "That girl we met at that wedding years ago. Lulu something or other."

"An unfortunate incident took his bride's life, so he is on the market again. And lucky you, Eugenia wants one of my girls to have first chance at claiming him."

"No thanks." Aimi wrinkled her nose.

"I'd rather mate with a human," Adi added.

Their mother's lips flattened. "One of you will claim him. There is nothing wrong with Harold that mouthwash won't fix."

"He's gross."

"And stupid."

"That's quite enough out of both of you. In case you hadn't noticed, you are running out of options. One more year, and you will be considered spinsters by our laws, and you know what that means."

It meant being subject to stupid Sept rules all in the name of preserving their race. She'd rather preserve her dignity, but that wasn't an option. But she could at least say no to Harold.

"I am not claiming Eugenia's son. If you want us to get mated, then bring us a decent option, and we'll reconsider."

"You know the options are limited." Limited because only sons born of certain lineages carrying a certain trait could be considered mates for the prestigious Silvergrace family. Barf. Aimi and Adi lacked the reverence for bloodlines that their mother and the rest of the family had.

"I don't see what the big deal is." Adi shrugged. "If we don't get married, then oh well. We'll do a turn with the milkshake and do our best to keep the battery industry hopping."

"How did I raise such ungrateful brats?" Their mother crossed her arms. "You do realize, if you don't marry, you will have to live with me forever." The fate of unmarried daughters in their family. Her mother smiled. "Did I mention my mother and her mother were incontinent by the age of seventy?"

Aimi's eyes widened. "No way. I am not wiping your ass, not when we can afford a nursemaid."

"Only if I let you hire one because, so long as I am the matriarch of this family, you won't have any money of your own other than what you earn or I give you."

"You are pure evil."

Her mother preened. "Thank you. Now, change into something pretty or don't. But I warn you, one of you will be claiming that young man."

Like hell. They didn't that day or the next when their mother tried to ambush them. Adi and Aimi played a game of 'dodge the marriage-bent mother' until garlicky Harold was safely claimed by some other poor girl looking to escape her overbearing matriarch.

But while the dodging game still proved as fun as it had when they'd started playing it at twenty-one, it did highlight one important fact. This was Aimi's last year to be considered a suitable bride. If she wanted a life outside this house and away from her family, then she needed to claim a man.

But not just any man.

A beast thought extinct. And, guess what, the world was outing them on a daily basis. Now, she just had to find the right one before her next birthday.

Chapter Three

Where to next?

City to city, he drifted, looking for clues as to where Parker kept Sue-Ellen stashed. It wasn't as if Uncle Theo hid. The man kept making appearances on news stations and gave speeches to Congress, but that didn't tell Brandon where his uncle lived.

Living as a transient meant it wasn't easy to come by information or even find a place he could stay for more than a few moments before being chased onward. The homeless under bridges wouldn't accept a monster in their midst. The sewers already had residents. The world where humans walked wasn't safe for him.

No one trusted the man with the monster face, which was why he stuck to rooftops, an observer to the madness now happening in the world. A madness punctuated by violence.

People, or more accurately humans, moved about in groups. Guns—now mostly stocked with silver bullets—hung on most hips. No one went around unarmed, not anymore. In this new world, everyone watched with suspicious eyes and twitchy trigger fingers.

Religion had made a resurgence, and the Bible thumpers screamed that the time had come. Thing was, the religions couldn't seem to agree on what that meant.

Months had passed since the initial reporting, months of people coming forward to say, "I have a furry side." Months of trying to understand what it all meant. Months of folks getting killed, lines being drawn, and blood being shed.

At the thought of blood, his stomach gurgled, hungry again, always hungry.

Ssshould go down there and have lunch. Crunch some bones.

The voice in his head, once so distinct, now sounded more and more like his own. The months of running had taken their toll. It was hard to spot the line separating man and beast, the fight to remain in control a constant one.

The fact that he'd had to rely more and more on his violent side to survive didn't help. Humans knew shifters existed, but that didn't make them automatically accepted.

The SHC had appointed a spokesperson to deal with the news of their existence. One guess on who was chosen for that role.

Uncle Parker. The same bastard who'd purposely maneuvered them into revealing their secret took the stage with a great big smile. He didn't do it alone. He brought out his trophy wife to show her off, her delicate humanity a political ploy meant to show the world that shifters could cohabit with humans. His children were of the perfect Stepford variety. Well groomed. Polite. Perfect poster children with a madman as a father.

Theo's immediate family wasn't the only one who made appearances with him. At times, Sue-

Ellen, the niece Theo had lovingly rescued—lying fucking bastard!—stood by his side with eyes downcast and hands clasped in front of her. She offered shy smiles to the cameras and soft words. The media loved her.

But the media also loved controversy, so for every photo-op they blasted across the networks trying to promote unity, they countered with the opposite, showing clips of animals versus men, where the men lost unless they used guns.

The world was in turmoil. Ever since the Great Reveal—a term he should note was spoken in hushed voices by shifters everywhere—Parker's words were played and replayed on all the news channels. News personalities kept asking the politicians in charge what they were going to do. Doctor Phil and other celebrities dissected what Theo said, and what he didn't say but possibly implied. People recited Theo's words on the street, trying to make sense of the revelation.

"My name is Theodore Parker, and I am here to tell you that, yes, shapeshifters do live among you. But despite what you might have seen, or think, you needn't fear. We're just like everybody else."

What a crock of shit.

"Our kind is, with a few exceptions where my company was trying to help, peaceful."

Whopper of a lie.

"We"—Parker drew Sue-Ellen close with a benevolent smile—"look forward to letting you learn about us." Ha. The only thing Parker was interested in learning was what it would take to control those making the laws.

As one of his former inner cadre, Brandon

knew what Parker was really after. He'd made his intentions quite clear. Being one of the hidden leaders of the SHC wasn't good enough for him. Theo wanted more power. Wanted a spot in the limelight. So he shoved all of his kind out of the fucking closet into the public eye.

Madman! Usually, people would have laughed and smiled and placated Theo while they waited for the men in the white coats to take him away.

Except there were videos. Damning videos, the ones showing the shifters' more feral sides. The clips of the battle at Bittech had brought a tidal wave of problems.

Violent animals attacking other animals. Beasts attacking humans.

Then there were the Bittech monsters—*like me*. More than a few had been caught on camera, their extra parts a source of fascinating horror.

Humanity felt threatened. Humans felt deceived.

The different became hunted. Which meant hunting right back. A man did what he had to in order to survive.

Lawmakers scrambled to accommodate this unexpected development. How to integrate this subset of the population? When someone was accused of a crime, what laws should they use, human or beast? If a wolf bit, was it assault, or did he need a muzzle like a dog?

And who were the animals in disguise? In this politically correct world, could prospective employers ask on their applications? Was it discrimination to not want a werewolf working in a chicken factory? Should it be a status on driver's licenses?

The suspicions of who might be hiding a wolf under their clothing caused many a person to seek medication for anxiety, and the sale of aluminum foil skyrocketed as paranoia reached new heights. As for the weapons industry, their stock shot to record heights, as everyone wanted to arm themselves.

Accusations flew, slapping anyone who seemed different. Innocents died as neighbor turned on neighbor.

All of Brandon's family and friends chose to move underground, and by that, he meant they'd left their home—a home they'd held for generations in the Everglades. They changed their names as they split up and slipped into mainstream society. They had to struggle extra hard to appear normal. To appear *human*.

Not everyone could fake it. Some of the older generation chose to go wild and take to the swamps. Even in there, though, Brandon was a freak. He couldn't hide easily, not with what Bittech had done to him.

And I can't hide, not while Parker has my sister. The slimy bastard kept hopping around the country spreading his bullshit 'Let's all live together' spiel. Eventually, Brandon would catch up to Theo, and when he did…

Crunch.

In the meantime, he had to survive. The fact that he lived, unchained and able to roam the world, didn't help him. It didn't make him normal again. When people saw him, they saw the monster.

They screamed.

He got annoyed.

Eat them. Fresh meat made a man—and his

reptile self—strong.

Too often he told his inner self—a now much colder, more cynical dark self—to calm the fuck down. No eating humans. But they did tempt him, especially when they smelled of chocolate. Being a monster had not diminished his sweet tooth.

As he crouched on a rooftop, a living gargoyle observing this new city, yet another place he couldn't blend in, he wondered why he even bothered to try.

Perhaps he should give up on finding answers or help for his monstrous dilemma. He should forget trying to regain normalcy and accept that this new look would stay with him forever. If he melted into the wilderness, went deep, deep into the woods and lived off the land, maybe he could stop the yearning. Perhaps, in time, he'd forget what it meant to be a man.

However, that would mean abandoning his sister, too.

With the rest of the family trying to keep themselves alive—and Wes doing his best to keep the special twins and Melanie out of science's reach—it left only Brandon who truly cared about one girl's fate.

Look at me, a real fucking hero. What a sad world he lived in when he was the last hope for his sister.

A whisper of sound alerted him to the fact that he shared the rooftop. He whirled and couldn't help but stare at the woman who stood behind him; willowy shaped, with long hair the color of moonlight, and eyes even stranger than his own. She canted her head to the side, perusing him.

It fascinated him that, even though she looked fully upon him, his features glaringly evident in the neon light of the sign overhead, she didn't run. She didn't scream. Inhaling deeply, she tilted her head back, revealing the smooth column of her throat.

Kill her now before she calls for help.

It would only take one bite of that smooth column. One bone-crunching chomp.

He shook his head. *No.* He wouldn't kill her, even if all his senses screamed that she meant danger.

Dangerous, how? All he could see was her fragile beauty—

The impact slammed him to the ground. The air *oomphed* out of him as her lithe figure landed atop him with more force and weight than expected. A hand, a strong hand tipped in opalescent claws, dug into his throat. Her eyes stared down at him, the orbs slitted and burning with green fire. Her almost pure-white hair lifted and danced around her head.

She was fucking hot. And on top of him, very much on top of him, and a part of him that hadn't played with anything other than his hand since the change stirred with interest.

"What's this roaming my city? A male, both unmarked and unclaimed," she whispered, dipping down low. "I should take you right now."

Perhaps she should. A certain part of him certainly thought so, and it didn't help that she squirmed atop him.

The fingers around his throat squeezed, yet no panic infused him. If he was meant to die, then so be it. He tired of hiding. He was also curious.

Who is ssshe? Even his dark half took interest. It still thought she was dangerous, but neither man nor beast could deny her allure.

Her lips hovered devastatingly close, the heat

of her breath warming his skin. "How did you come here? Tell me your name."

A name? What name should he give her? The one he'd started in the world with no longer seemed to fit. He was more than just a simple Brandon and, at the same time, less than the naïve man he used to be.

"My name is…" Ace? No, he wouldn't use Ace either. That was Andrew's rude misnomer, the other madman involved in the genetic experiments at Bittech.

What did that leave?

"I am no one, and I come from…" *Don't spread your taint to a town already devastated.* "Nowhere. Who are you? What are you?" Because she smelled like him, but…different.

Ssmells yummy.

Very yummy. As in he wanted to lick her from head to toe yummy.

"What do you mean, what am I?" Her brow crinkled. "I am the same thing you are." Her shoulders drew back, her head tilted imperially, and for a moment, shadowy wings glistened silver at her back. "We are dragon."

At her serious claim, he gaped then snorted before he outright laughed.

"Why are you giggling?" She seemed perturbed at his reaction.

"Men don't giggle. We guffaw. And I'm guffawing because that is the most ridiculous thing I've heard. I'm no dragon. I'm nothing anymore but a fucking mess." Bitter words for a bitter fate.

"What is your family name? Who are you descended from?"

Was there any point in hiding? It wasn't as if anyone used his name anymore. "Mercer."

"Never heard of them. Are you from the European contingent?"

"More like Florida, and not from any hoity-toity pack or family either. Just one of several gators my ma popped out." He shrugged. "I'm not even the biggest. Wes has got like half an inch on me."

"You are not making any sense. There are no dragons in Florida on account of the seadrakes. They're very territorial."

"Listen, moonbeam, I think you might have forgotten to take your meds this morning. Dragons aren't real."

"But by your own words you believe in shifters?" Her lips quirked.

"Of course, because I am one, and given your lovely claws, I'm guessing you're one, too."

"No, I am dragon."

"Sure you are, and even if I believed you, dragons are still shifters."

"Don't let my mother hear you say that. She'll wash your mouth out with castor oil."

"Does your mother know you escaped your room?" A padded room he'd wager, given her delusion. Dragons. Really? He might be funny looking, but he wasn't gullible.

"I don't need permission to roam this city. Especially not from my mother."

"What about your father?"

"I don't have one anymore."

"Let me guess, he was a dragon, too." He couldn't stop the smirk.

"As a matter of fact, he was. We lost him to a

plane accident."

"So, what, did he fly into a propeller?"

"Of course, not. It was a small Cessna plane, and it got caught in some cross winds and crashed. According to Mother, he was probably so worried about outing himself that he didn't abandon the craft and take flight." She shook her head. "Usually, he would have healed any injuries sustained, but I don't think he counted on the plane exploding when it landed."

Her fantasy world deepened, and he couldn't help but feed it. "So, your daddy was a dragon. And what of your mother."

She rolled her eyes. "Dragon, too, of course. It is the only way to make one."

"Of course, it is." Had to admire the depth of her delusion.

"We will make some fine dragonlings to carry the family name."

Choke. What? "Slow down, moonbeam. We won't be making nothing because you seem to have forgotten I'm not a dragon."

She leaned down and sniffed. "You smell like one."

"What I smell like is a man on the run whose skin hasn't seen anything but lakes and rivers in weeks. Let me assure you, I am most definitely not a dragon." Or daddy material.

Curiosity shone in her gaze as she cocked her head. "Then what are you if not dragon?"

"I'm what happens when science goes wild. The man the world knows as Parker—"

"You know Parker?"

"Unfortunately." He grimaced. "He's my

uncle."

"What?" She jumped to her feet, a grip on his shirt pulling him up after her, impressive given he wasn't a lightweight. Although, he should note that he wasn't as heavy as he used to be. A lack of proper meals did that to a man. "You're related to that whoreson? I didn't know he was a dragon. I thought he was some kind of low-born lizard."

"Not right on either account. He's a wolf. My aunt married outside the family. Apparently, she had a thing for dogs."

Her lips pursed. "I can see you have interesting lineage. You may not want to mention that to my mother or aunts. We need them to think you're a suitable mate if this is going to work."

"I am a freak, not suitable for anything, let alone being someone's mate." He grabbed hold of her wrists, noting the fine bones, and pried her fingers from his shirt. She might be strong, but he was happy to note that he proved stronger.

What he couldn't have prepared for was how dirty she'd play. She grabbed him by the junk, firmly too, and leaned up to snap, "You will not speak of yourself with such disparagement anymore. Have some pride in your genes."

"Even if they're not mine?"

"You're not making any sense. Of course, they're yours. Dragons are born, not made."

His turn to shake his head and resist an urge to punch her for squishing his balls. Bayou born and bred didn't mean he was an asshat who hit girls.

"All of what you see is science-made, except for the cock you're squeezing. That's all me." And *me* was not exactly hating being touched. How long since he'd been this close to a woman?

"You can impress me with your virility later once I've claimed you before witnesses."

"You lost me."

"Good thing I'm smart enough to think for us both. Just do as you're told, and it will all be fine. Better than fine. I think we shall do quite well together. Unlike that idiot Harold, you smell nice, and you're handsome, too." She patted his cheek.

Yeah, so a part of him wanted to snort and mock her calling him handsome. But...

Another part of him practically rolled on its back and purred. Fucking purred. It was utterly emasculating.

"For the last time. I'm not a dragon."

"Fine. You're not. We can discuss what you are later. We should get out of here before I have to deal with my cousins. This building is in their territory, which is why it's so much fun to pop in for a visit and leave them a present."

The girl he'd called moonbeam took a step away and dug into a pocket. She pulled out a figurine of a pretty princess in some yellow frock, holding up an index finger. The detail was incredible. The fact that she was leaving it to taunt even more astonishing.

"Do you often screw with your cousins?"

"Every chance I get."

Sshe is perfect. Devious and sexy. The most deadly of combinations.

Sporting a pleased smirk, she stepped back from the tiny effigy. "Now that I've left a calling card, time for you to change so we can go."

"I don't have a shirt. These things make it

kind of hard to find one that fits." His wings rustled, and he noted how her gaze followed the play of muscles across his bared chest. The ends of a scarf, wrapped around his neck, dangled down. Winter fast approached, and he needed to move west to stay ahead of it.

As time marched on and he lost touch with his humanity, the more he noticed how temperature affected him. Cool temps put him right to sleep—and chapped his skin. He now traveled with lube, the good kind that doubled for when his hand got used during extra-curricular activities.

Hot temperatures made him relax and smile. He likened it to a big joint, and just like with Mary Jane, he got the munchies, too—for raw meat.

No matter the weather conditions, though, he remained alert. It was the only way to ensure survival. Whether sleepy or high, if he had to spring into action, he went from relaxed to adrenalized in an instant.

"I wasn't talking about putting a shirt on. With a body like that, I say show it off. But we can't walk around while you're in your hybrid form. You shouldn't even be playing in the city limits wearing it." Her eyes widened. "Are you a rule breaker? A trailblazer? Justice warrior?"

"No."

"A shame." She seemed almost disappointed.

"I am dangerous to be around, though, so you should probably leave and forget you saw me."

Again, she uttered that enchanting laughter. The chime of bells in the wind, the sound tickled across his exposed skin, warming him despite the cool evening air.

"Forget you? Never. Now that I've found you, you're mine."

Mine. How nice that sounded. But it also reminded him of his time at Bittech. "I belong to no one."

"You say that now…but you'll change your mind." She smiled and winked. "I guess if I'm going to claim you, I should know your first name because it seems a little odd for me to call you by your last."

"You can call me Ace." The name of the monster that did Bittech's dirty deeds.

She rejected it. "That is infantile and won't do at all. Do you have another name? A more proper one that Mother might approve of?"

As if he cared what her mother thought of him. He wasn't even sure he cared what *she* thought. Except…he kind of did. She was the first person to truly speak to him in a while. He'd stopped calling his family, unable to listen to their pleas to come join them despite the danger he'd bring. Unable to deal with their belief that Sue-Ellen was fine and didn't need rescue.

Sue-Ellen wouldn't be fine until he got her away from Parker.

Instead of replying, he turned the query back on her. "What's your name? Seems only fair you spill first since you're the one keen on knowing."

She tossed her head, the movement causing her hair to undulate in a wave of silver. "My name is Aimi Silvergrace, daughter of Zahra and Tobin. My mother is the Contessa for the Silver Sept."

"Sounds like you come from money."

"I do. We're rich. Filthy rich, and I should warn that my mother prides herself on being an upper-class snob."

"Mine makes the best crab chowder in the bayou."

"She can cook? A peasant endeavor, but intriguing. When we visit, we shall allow her to cook for me."

Allow? And what was with the "When we visit?" There was no *we*. "I thought I'd made myself clear. I want nothing to do with you."

She shot him a gaze that said without words what a foolish boy he was. "You want me."

"Do not."

"You are a horrible liar. My whole family is going to eat you alive."

"This might sound like an odd question, but to be clear, do you mean that literally?" Because the more he chatted with Aimi of the moonbeam hair, and even more flighty ideas, the more he was convinced she was fucking nuts. He should also note that he had more than one aunt who would eat their guests and bury their bones. His aunt Tanya was famous for her Frenemy Soup.

"The only one who will actually eat you will be me." She licked her lips, and the wink left nothing to the imagination.

He might have shuddered—because of the cold. Nothing else.

She's right. I am a shitty liar.

She clapped her hands. "Enough idle chitchat. We can indulge in that later at the house. Change back to your human guise and let us get moving. I'm curious to see how you appear. You're not ridiculously hideous, are you? Then again, I guess it doesn't matter that much. We could always screw in the dark. Or you could wear this face." She patted his cheek. "This face is handsome. But it should only be worn in private." She gave him a harder tap. "And I mean in private with me. Now, stop playing and change. I am sure you are taxing your strength holding this form for so long."

"I can't change."

"What do you mean you can't?"

Nothing like having to admit his deficiency. He rolled his big shoulders. "Like I keep trying to tell you, I'm broken. Actually, according to Bittech and the doctors there, they 'improved' me. They took a simple swamp gator from the wrong side of town and made me into some kind of super breed. There is a catch, though. This is the only thing I can be now. This hideous monster shape."

Not ugly, beautiffful. His inner self took exception, and his wings fluttered, an outward push by his reptile half. The pushes were getting harder and harder to control, and at times, he wondered why he bothered fighting at all.

"You cannot change?" Her fine brows pulled tight. "At all?"

"Nope. This is me, moonbeam. Not a guy you should be bringing home to meet Mom. I am nothing but a mistake."

Chapter Four

He didn't say it for pity, more as an apology, but Aimi couldn't understand why he persisted in his belief that he was a mistake.

There was undoubtedly something different about him, something exotic that came from more than just the incredible beauty and control he had over his hybrid shape. Only the strongest could maintain a half-shift for any length of time. It almost made her giggle with glee at her fortuitous finding of him. Who would have thought her middle-of-the-night wanderings would bring her in contact with an eligible male?

A strong mate that will not only get my mother off my back but also send my sisters and cousins into total green meltdown.

A sweet victory.

Except he didn't seem keen on hooking up. She doubted it had to do with her looks—it wasn't vanity that said she was pretty. The mirror said it, too.

She detected no mark on him, no prior claim, so it wasn't as if he couldn't accept Aimi as his mate. And she'd not imagined the erection.

He is attracted to me but thinks he's not worthy. Understandable. She was pretty freaking awesome.

She forgave him his awe. "I told you before, I won't tolerate you denigrating yourself. It is unseemly in a dragon. And I think we should address the fact that your attitude indicates you believe the world revolves around you. Not anymore it doesn't." She tilted her chin and angled her nose in the air as her mother had taught her. "I am the center of the universe. More specifically, *your* universe." She fixed him with a stare. He was also her ticket out of the house and from under her mother's rule. First, though, she needed to properly claim him in front of witnesses.

She grabbed his hand and tugged him in the direction of the door leading to the rooftop stairs. "Let's go."

"We can't go. At least, I can't. I rarely travel the streets like this. Too dangerous." Silver bullets were a bitch to heal from.

"I admit your hybrid shape might make it more complicated to pass unnoticed, but only until we reach my car a few blocks away."

"And where do you plan to take me?"

"Home, of course. It's about an hour's drive from here. The condo would be closer, but nobody's there right now. Besides, if we go to our house in the 'burbs, I'll wager my Aunt Xylia has something to help you. Just don't trust anything from Waida. She tends to add little extras." Sometimes, those extras refused to leave. Not everyone wanted a third nipple, and Uncle Jerome never forgave his sister for that.

Her future mate planted his feet and refused to move to the rooftop door. He was so adorably stubborn. She'd have to talk to her mother about breaking him of that habit. Not that her mother had had much luck with Aimi's father. Her mother had tried to cage Aimi's dad, but he refused to stay home safe with the hoard—and she meant a real hoard. All dragons had one, the size of it determined by their dwelling. Mother's was massive. Aimi had one started, but it was starting to outgrow her closet. She'd have to bargain for more room.

Or I could just move out with my mate. Get their own place in the city. With extra bedrooms for her treasures.

"I'm not going anywhere with you."

A heavy sigh blew past her lips. "Again with the word 'no.' World. Me." She punctuated the words with a swirl of a finger around her head. Poor, simple guy. He'd learn. Speaking of which… "Hey, you still haven't given me your name. And don't give me something foolish again like Ace. That's for gangsters, not someone who is about to join with the Silvergrace family." And father a few babies that would finally get her mother off her back—"When are you going to stop being so picky and settle down with a dragon lord and ensure the continuation of our line?"

Guess what, Mother. You're about to get your wish.

"My real name is Brandon. Does that work for you, moonbeam?"

She smiled. "It does, although I prefer Brand. It's got more presence. I also find your nickname for me acceptable. What's less acceptable is your stubborn refusal to obey."

"It's not stubborn. I am not a dog to be ordered around."

"You don't like orders, then fine. I am asking you to come with me." She struggled but managed to utter, "Please."

"Still not happening. Up here, no one can see me, which means, no dodging bullets."

"But dodging danger is what makes life so entertaining. It also keeps us fit."

"Bullets make holes."

"You'll heal."

"I'd rather not, which is why I'm going to stay here, and you're going to leave." He gave her a little shove. "Vamoose." Another nudge. "*Adios.*" A wave of his hand. "Don't let the door hit you on the ass."

Realization hit her. "How is it that you're displaying alpha tendencies? I thought that trait had been bred out of our kind centuries ago." Then again, her father wasn't all that docile when Mother wasn't around.

"It's called having balls, moonbeam. I might have had a lot done to me, but I still have them." To her shock, he grabbed his groin and gave it a squeeze.

It was ridiculously masculine. Stranger still, she enjoyed it. "With your alpha nature and my impeccable genes, do you realize what kind of daughters we're going to have?"

"Daughters?"

"I'd prefer a few sons. That would really cement our place in the Silver Sept."

"Sons?" he squeaked for a second time.

How cute. Maybe she'd been mistaken about him being alpha. A beta would work a lot better with her lifestyle. They tended to ask fewer questions. At least, Caelly's beta husband, Soren, tended to be mellow and just stay at home with the kids. But not all males were like that.

"Yes, sons. The Silvergraces are plagued by daughters. And sisters." She couldn't help but frown.

"Do you have sisters?"

"One sister, and some brothers."

"Brothers, really?" She brightened. "Are they single?"

"No."

"Pity. Then again, it doesn't matter. I'd rather keep you and your possible boy-making genes to myself. No use in sharing that kind of prestige with others."

"That seems rather mercenary."

"What do you expect of dragons?" She slipped around him to his back. She ran a finger over his wings—fascinating things. She'd never seen full-sized wings on a hybrid before. "How do you manage these? Most dragons who can hold a half-shift have a hard time with these. They're usually stunted or spastic in their movements. You have great control." A control that wavered, given the wings shivered as she stroked along a tendon, following it to where it merged seamlessly into his back. She slid her arms around him, under the wings, her fingers tickling over his flat and ridged stomach. "A pretty adornment, and yet such a waste given they're useless." The hybrid shapes were good only for fighting short battles, not flight.

"How is flying useless?"

She froze against him. "Did you say fly? You fly in this shape?" Impossible. Only in their dragon shape could they manage flight. "Show me."

"You'd have to stop hugging me first."

But she didn't want to stop. Brand was hers, and she wanted to touch him. To mark him for the world to see. *He's mine.* A new treasure for her hoard. *My shiny.*

She ducked around his wings and faced him, fascinated by his proud bearing, her senses tingling at the scent of him. She traced her fingers across his jaw, and he pulled away.

"Don't."

"Why not?"

"I'm not a freak for you to grope."

"Who called you a freak? I think you're quite handsome." So handsome even in this shape that she stood on tiptoe and gave him a light kiss, a fleeting press of skin that ignited something between them.

Mine.

The very fact that Aimi coveted him so desperately meant she stepped away. She was the one in control here, not him.

"Why did you do that?" He crossed his arms and glared.

"Because I felt like it." Instinct wanted her to touch him. But her desire for him didn't make her gullible. "I don't believe you can fly. Not in this shape. That is a feat reserved for when we are dragon."

"Except…" The powerful muscles of his thighs strained against his khaki slacks as he leaped upward. "I." Flutter. "Am not." Flap." A dragon."

Each stroke of his wings took him higher into the air until he hovered about fifteen feet above.

"Amazing." She breathed the word. "You will make a fine husband." A strong mate.

"Actually, I'm the fly-away groom. It was nice meeting you, moonbeam. Best of luck on trapping some poor bastard into being your Stepford husband."

And then he thought to fly away from her,

this male who'd come into her world unmarked and unclaimed. He taunted her with his existence then mocked her by escaping, expecting her to chase.

It was just like the mating dances of old when her kind flew the skies, owning the heavens and the lands underneath. The good old days that were now long gone. These days, dragons hid themselves. They had to after the great hunts of the Middle Ages decimated their numbers. Stupid kings sending their knights on constant quests to defeat the mighty beasts. They were hunted almost to extinction during that dark era.

But that had been hundreds of years ago. Now, the dragons thrived and accumulated wealth, pretty-shiny piles of it all over the world.

People could say money didn't bring happiness. They'd obviously never rolled in gold dust, silky soft and warm to the skin.

Yet for all the joys, she had to be careful. The dragons no longer ruled the heavens in the cities. They needed to employ caution and stealth. There were times it sucked. Times it proved a challenge to obey.

But challenge was a fun thing. The hunt she was about to embark on even better.

Hands on her hips, Aimi watched her male fly away and smiled.

They are all going to be so jealous when they see who I snagged.

If she could find him.

A few hours later, having returned home to gather intel, Aimi scowled over Adrianne's shoulder. "What do you mean you can't track him?"

Much as she'd wanted to keep her finding of a

male dragon secret, she'd had to confide in someone because, with Brandon taking to the skies, it meant he didn't leave a trail.

Playing hard to get. How cute. It would make her claiming all the more satisfying—after she stopped hitting him for making it so difficult. Why couldn't he just obey?

Her biggest fear now was that one of her cousins, or even her aunts, would find him first.

He's mine. And she wanted him bad enough that she'd give up part of her treasure to keep him.

Adi popped the purple lollipop out of her mouth, displaying for a second her purple tongue and inner lip. "Whoever this guy is that you claim you found, he is either really, really good at hiding, or he doesn't exist."

"Who doesn't exist?" Aunt Xylia made no pretense of ignoring their conversation as she snuck up behind them in the library.

By library, Aimi should note that it spanned several stories, the ceiling a domed cupola with skylights. UV-protected ones, of course, to protect the thousands of books stored, many of them ancient and bound in treated skin—not all of it animal.

Everything from long-lost scrolls to ancient scriptures to the latest in werewolf romance filled the space. They especially enjoyed reading supposed dragon romances. The fact that none of those authors got their culture right was giggle worthy.

"You still haven't answered," her aunt snapped, leaning closer.

Adi tried to swap screens, but Aimi knew there was no point in hiding their research. Especially not from Aunt Xylia; the aunt she hoped could help

Brand with his problem.

Aimi straightened her shoulders and blurted, "I found a mate today."

"Found one?" Her aunt straightened and arched a finely groomed brow. "You don't just 'find' a mate. They don't just drop out of the sky."

"This one did. And I claimed him." Mostly. She'd put the mark on him as soon as she located him again.

"You claimed a man that fell out of the sky? Wonderful. Your mother will be pleased. Although, she will stand to lose that sweet new ride she commissioned."

It did not surprise Aimi that her mother had bet against her. If Aimi could have bet on herself not getting hitched, she would have, but apparently, that was considered cheating or something in the marriage pool.

"I did find a mate, and a strong one, too. He can hold a hybrid shape."

"For what? A minute. Two? Your grandfather used to be able to hold it for almost an hour. It's how he made his money in the boxing rings back in the forties that started our family back on the road to prosperity."

The Depression had hit everyone hard, but they'd also had to deal with a dragon hunter who caught on to the dragon's existence. He'd gone after every asset the Silvergraces owned when he couldn't get to them directly. They'd eventually dealt with him, but not without cost to their fortune. A fortune that was bigger and better today.

"Mine can hold his shape even longer." So long, he apparently couldn't change back, but she didn't feel a need to reveal that aspect yet.

"Really?" The doubting tone drew out the word.

"Yes, really."

"And where is this incredible paragon?"

"You'll meet him soon."

"Sure, we will." Her aunt's gaze fixed on her. "You do know just claiming you're mated doesn't count. You actually have to produce a male and prove it before you can be relieved of your duties to the family."

"He exists." Somewhere.

"Then I look forward to meeting him."

Aimi and Adi watched their aunt make her way to the door and waited until they were sure she was gone before huddling heads and whispering.

"I think she's on to us."

"She'd have to be stupid not to be," Adi snorted. "Now, back to this imaginary mate of yours. Where do you think he might have gone next?"

"I don't know."

And hours later, sitting on the roof of her house, she still didn't know. However, oddly enough, she wasn't worried. Despite their short encounter, she could have sworn a bond had been forged between them. A tenuous one for the moment, but it was there, inside her, a slender thread linking them. Tomorrow, she would use to it to track down her missing mate.

I will find him and claim him. Then she was shopping for a new home to stash her hoard.

Chapter Five

I found her.

The crazy woman with moonbeam hair sat with her knees tucked under her chin, perched on the roof of a house—if, by house, something with a few wings and more square footage than a mall counted.

He'd wondered if he had the right place when he saw it during his first pass overhead. It wasn't as if the woman he'd met on the rooftop had given him an address, just a name. *Aimi Silvergrace,* a name both beautiful and suiting. A name he'd used to track down information—a quick swoop across a balcony, swiping a smartphone as he passed, gave him access to internet search.

There wasn't a ton of information about her. Moonbeam didn't belong to social media. However, she didn't entirely escape the news, given she was an heiress of a very old, aristocratic family. She attended things like fundraisers and opera events. One article described her family as "filthy rich." And snobby. The bluest blood you could imagine—and yet she'd been rooftop slumming when she'd found him.

Found me and claimed I was a dragon. She also claimed I am hers.

Because she isss mine. The coldness of his heart couldn't help him from thinking it. Feeling it. It was utter nonsense, of course.

Dragons didn't exist, and no one wanted a monster. She played games with him, obviously. But why? He wanted to know. Wanted to know why she lied. Why she tortured him.

Just like a tiny spark of hope within wanted to know if, perhaps, she spoke the truth. Were there others like him?

To find out, he'd have to see her again. He didn't question the urgency of this need. He forgot for a moment the plight of his sister. Only one thing mattered: finding Aimi.

So he located her, and without calling first or warning, he sought her out. He hovered far overhead, a tiny speck in the grand scheme of things, yet she spotted him. She peered upward and looked right at him.

How did she know he was there? *The same way I knew where to go.* Much like a homing pigeon—super tasty when basted over a coal-driven fire—he just knew where she was. He dipped a little lower, allowing her to see him clearly. He remained aloft, though, not sure if he dared come within reach.

Showoff.

The voice wasn't his own, and yet…it was in his head, and distinctly feminine. He whirled around to look, but he remained alone in the sky.

Can you hear me? She spoke; not aloud, but inside his head again. *If you can, then you might want to get down here before they set them loose.*

"Set what loose?" he spoke the words he thought aloud.

The perimeter drones. You set off an alarm as soon as you entered our airspace.

What alarm? He'd not touched a damned thing. His wings flapped, slow and steady as he peered around. "I don't see anything." Did she screw with the yokel from the swamp?

Again with the stubborn not listening. Don't say I didn't warn you.

The spoken thought had barely finished when he heard the hum of a small engine. Whipping from the west perimeter, the matte-painted drone zipped quickly toward Brandon, the only true indication of its presence a pinprick of red light, a laser sight locked on his chest.

Shit.

He flapped his wings and drew himself higher, yet the drone's aim remained locked to his body. He'd have to prove trickier if he were to stay out of harm's way.

Flattening, he arrowed toward it. The red dot hit him in the forehead. Brandon stretched his arms wide.

What are you doing? She sounded curious rather than worried.

Doing what any boy did when presented with a cool toy. He wanted to play.

The drone didn't seem sure what to do. Good news, though, it didn't fire. Which meant it wasn't really interested in killing him.

The whirring machine didn't move as he reached out to snag it.

Zap, a hot streak of fire kissed a wing at his back, and he hissed.

Fuckers had a second one on the move. The first one played dead as a decoy.

There's a third one coming in from above.

The warning sounded amused. He, on the other hand, wasn't. He wasn't used to being challenged in the sky. Bittech never truly taught their experiments any avian tactics. It was considered enough that they *could* fly.

But now, as Brandon zipped back and forth, up and down, dodging streaks of fire, he really wished he had a gun and had learned to shoot.

Alas, all he had was himself. And an audience.

Way to impress the girl. Nothing screamed, "I'm a stud" like getting harassed by small robots.

The good news about the bots, which now swarmed him—a dozen by his last count—was they still seemed to be more intent on herding him down to the courtyard than actually killing him.

Of course, they're not going to kill you. Yet.

"Not reassuring," he muttered aloud.

Then you should have come with me earlier. We could have avoided some of this.

"Can't you call them off?"

Nope. The defense system is automated. Just land in the courtyard. But don't let anyone touch you. I'll be there in a minute.

The words registered, but he didn't reply, given the drones harried him, urging him to the massive roundabout area at the front of the mansion.

He landed a few paces in front of a spouting fountain, a massive one featuring—no surprise— sculpted dragons that spewed water from their mouths. Very cool looking and much less daunting than the welcoming committee.

The tips of his scarf weren't enough to cover his shirtless torso from the avid stares of the women gathered, their ages varying, and yet many of them sported the same silvery hair as Aimi. They also all had freakish eyes, the vertical slits glowing with green fire as they unabashedly eyed him head to toe.

He crossed his arms over his chest and glared, daring them to do something: scream, panic, call him a monster, shoot.

Instead, one of the younger girls with her hair cut in a short, wispy style exclaimed, "It's a boy."

"Don't you mean a man?" The woman wearing dark eyeliner and hair in platinum curls smiled. "A very yummy and strong man."

"Who do you belong to?" asked an older woman, her silvery strands bound up in a chignon that drew emphasis to the lean column of her neck.

"He belongs to me!" The claim came from Aimi, who emerged from the house in a quick walk. He couldn't deny being happy to see her again—she was intriguing. What he didn't understand was the spurt of warmth her words caused.

I belong to no one. Not Bittech. Not his uncle. And most certainly not this slip of a girl.

"Moonbeam. Fancy seeing you again." When in doubt, pretend extreme nonchalance. He'd learned that lesson from a big cat in captivity at Bittech. The felines had insouciance down to an art.

"This is your mate? The one you told me about?" The woman with the bun laughed. "I'll be damned. You weren't lying. He is strong."

"And mine." Aimi moved to stand between the women and Brandon. "So claws off, or I'll eat your face."

"Don't I get a say?" he asked.

"No." The word met laughter.

"He speaks!"

"He can fly!"

"I say we tackle her and snare him," whispered another.

"Touch my sister, and I'll wipe out your bank accounts," said another girl, her hair punked out, her arms crossed over her chest.

"Moonbeam," he murmured, leaning close. "What the hell is going on here? Who are these people?"

"Family. I warned you they'd eat you alive. Don't worry. I'll keep you safe. I just need to make your status clear."

"My status?"

"As my soon-to-be mate. Trust me. It's best this way."

"Best for whom? What do I get out of this?"

She smiled, and he would have agreed to anything to keep her smiling at him forever. "You get me."

That worked, too. As soon as he felt himself falling under her crazy spell, he snapped out of it. "What's the alternative? One of them?" He indicated the horde still eyeing him and, in some cases, still discussing whether or not to steal him.

Aimi turned her head to peek at him over her shoulder. "You're mine. If they touch you, family or not, I will have to maim them."

"And what if I touch them? What happens to me?"

"Why would you touch them when you have this?" She let her hands skim her frame. "I'm not worried. Have you so soon forgotten your world now revolves around me?"

Would that be such a bad thing? Just being

with her so far had been the best thing to happen to Brandon in what seemed like forever. He couldn't remember the last time he'd felt so adrenalized and warm and happy; a true happy that came from within and not a heated chimneystack.

At the same time, with his fascination for Aimi, came a dereliction in his quest. Look at where he was because he'd chased a moonbeam. He'd not left town as planned. Not gone looking for clues about his sister but rather put all his efforts in tracking down a crazy woman.

A crazy woman who wants me.

He tried to distract himself from her and return to the situation at hand. "So you're related to all these women."

"Was it the hair that gave it away?" stated a girl wearing a no-nonsense pantsuit and glasses.

"Ah, look at that, he's pretty and not completely stupid," snickered another in the crowd.

Funny, because he felt pretty damned dumb, and confused. Why did they call him pretty? Were they all blind to the fact that he wore the face and body of a monster?

"I guess I should do introductions." Aimi returned to his side and tucked her hand on his bicep—causing him to suck in a breath—and pointed with the other. "That's my Aunt Xylia wearing the bun. And Aunties Valda and Vanna at the back." She pointed to a pair of women wearing glasses and cardigans who nodded at him. "Then there's my sister Adrianne with the funky hair. And those are my cousins, Deka and Babette."

"You all live here?"

"Yes. There's more of us actually. But you can

meet them later."

"You still haven't told us who this handsome man is," Deka said, batting her lashes in his direction.

"Claws off, or I'll pull them for you. This is Brand, and he's mine."

"I don't see a mark," noted Babette.

"Because I was waiting for witnesses."

"We can witness."

Aimi shook her head. "I want Mother here to see it."

"Then you'll have to wait, as your mother is out of town until tomorrow sometime," Xylia noted.

"Good. That gives us time to deal with a few issues."

"You mean like the one where you keep trying to claim me?" He ducked low enough to whisper it against her ear, feeling the silken brush of her hair against his lips.

"Would you prefer me or someone else?"

"You'd give me a choice?"

"No. And now, do you mind waiting to discuss this later? We have an audience." An audience that was smirking.

"I want to know what's going on." Because he felt as if he'd walked into a different dimension. Nothing since he'd met Aimi had unfolded as expected.

"You're an unclaimed male, and I want you as my mate. That's all there is to it."

"I'd say there's a bit more, such as my consent."

"You do know I don't need it, right?"

"I disagree."

"Then find a way to rewrite the laws. As it

stands, my claiming you is the way of the dragon." The enigmatic reply didn't get expanded as she began to walk towards the house, the other women having already turned around to return inside.

He hesitated, not having been specifically invited to follow, and yet, at the same time, still in need of answers, such as why all these women seemed to regard him as normal. Did they not notice the scales and the wings?

And why did they keep calling him a hybrid? Were there others who'd been spliced and diced into something new like him?

Aimi stopped at the top step of the porch—if a grand staircase of stone tiered with precision could have such a banal name. She peeked over her shoulder at him. "Are you going to stand there all night, or are you coming inside?"

"What happens inside?"

"Come in and find out." She stepped through the front door, leaving him alone.

What to do? His body still stung from the nicks of fire the drones had inflicted. He was hungry, his last stolen meal over a day ago. Fatigue pulled at every single one of his muscles. It had taken a lot to find moonbeam. She lived well outside the city limits, which meant lots of flight time. All the ailments of his body, though, paled before the most insistent thing: his curiosity.

It was curiosity—and a strange need to see Aimi again—that had driven him to locate her and then come find her. Now that he was here, would he let a simple thing like uncertainty stop him?

Hell, no. He'd survived worse than a few silver-haired women.

So he followed, but he managed only one step over the threshold when a voice barked, "You can drop the hybrid shape now. You and Aimi have made your point. You're strong. But we wear our human shapes in the house. It's easier on the hardwood floors."

Aimi came to his defense before he could explain. "So, we have a teeny-tiny problem. Brand over here is having a bit of an issue switching back. We were hoping you could give him a hand with that, Aunt Xylia."

"Stuck?" Xylia's eyes widened in surprise. "I've never heard of that."

"Not all that unusual. It happens to shifters who've lost touch with their humanity." Dressed bohemian style with a beaded necklace—comprised of tiny skulls—a new woman came into view.

Before he could open his mouth and explain his situation, Aimi elbowed him. He clamped his lips shut and glared at her, not that she noticed, given she faced her aunt.

Aimi shrugged. "Maybe he ate something he shouldn't have. I was hoping Aunt Xylia had something in her apothecary to help?"

"Or I could take him home with me." The hippy lady eyed him.

Aimi shook her head. "No thanks. We're good, Aunt Waida. Aunt Xylia surely has something right here."

The lady with the bun nodded. "I might. Come with me."

"Yeah, better get him fixed, or your honeymoon is gonna be rough," snickered one of the cousins.

"Your jealousy warms me," Aimi sassed back. "Later." A benign reply punctuated with a pair of raised middle fingers over her shoulders as she followed the swaying skirt of her aunt.

"I saw that," said Xylia. "What have we told you about language in the house?"

"It's the twenty-first century. Don't you think it's time we loosened the girdle?"

"No, and we should never have let our skirts go above our ankles either."

As the aunt and niece squabbled over new-generation values versus old, he found himself taking in the mansion he'd entered. It intimidated, reminding him that he was just a small-town boy. A poor one at that, from the wrong side of the swamp.

I don't belong here.

He'd seen wealth during his time incarcerated at Bittech, knew what kind of privilege came with money. The men who flaunted it—Andrew and Parker and the other scum running the Bittech scam—were paupers compared to the lavish lifestyle displayed here.

White marble floors lined the massive hallway, a hallway that should have had a map, given it had branches going off left and right and, in between those branches, opulent rooms, at least from what he could see through open doors.

They walked for a while alongside fluted archways that framed the interior of a conservatory lush with plants and the tinkling sound of a water feature. Then there was the corridor that flanked the dining hall. He'd never imagined a table could stretch so long or host so many chairs.

"Do you ever eat in there?"

Aimi didn't even glance to the side. "That's the formal dining room. We use it about three or four times a year when we receive visitors or are celebrating a mating."

"And you fill those seats?"

"Easily and with spillover. We usually have the young ones using the regular dining chamber that sits fifty more."

"How big is your family?"

"You'll see. We probably won't have time to gather them for our ceremony, but I'm sure Mother will have the invitations out to a reception before the week's end to introduce you to the Sept families."

She spoke as if he'd stick around. Not likely. A monster like him would bring too much attention. The world was a place gone mad. The last thing he wanted to do was bring the monster hunters here.

If they dare to strike, then I'll protect. Crunch some bones. Break some necks.

His cold, inner self had no qualms about doing what had to be done. But Brandon didn't want to give in. Giving in to the cold meant losing what was left of him: the brother who just wanted to do the right thing. The boy from the swamp, who had plans to not follow in family footsteps and end up in jail but to go to community college and learn a trade.

Instead, he'd learned pain, subterfuge, and intimidation as Bittech forced him to do their bidding. A command that usually involved doing nasty things to others.

That was then. This is now.

Aimi's voice tickled at him, and he ignored it, trying to pretend she hadn't just read his mind.

"Where exactly are we going?" And should he

leave a trail of breadcrumbs behind, a valid wonder as they wound down some stairs, the distance a few levels at least underground?

"Auntie keeps her lab down here."

"A lab." He froze. "She's a doctor?" Someone who liked to poke people with needles and inject them with liquid fire? Oh, hell no.

"Don't insult me, boy. Humans use doctors. I am a true alchemist."

"Which, in today's world, would be known as a drug dealer," Aimi sagely advised.

Smack.

The cuff by her aunt caused Aimi to glare. "Don't slap me for telling the truth. You do peddle drugs, just not only the hallucinogenic kind. She does medicines, too."

He refused to budge, and his lips flattened. "I don't do drugs."

The violet eyes of the aunt perused him, the slitted part of her orbs flashing with green fire. "No drugs? Then am I to assume you are content remaining in your hybrid shape?"

Of course, he fucking wasn't. But what she asked of him... "You don't understand. Drugs and doctors playing with my DNA are what got me into this mess."

"Then perhaps drugs can get you out."

Doubtful. The damage had occurred at a cellular level. "I don't think this is a good idea." He turned around and made to retrace his steps. "I should leave."

"I am ashamed of you, niece. You chose a coward as a mate." The disdain shone in the words.

"He's not a coward," Aimi retorted. "Just

wary."

"Hesitation is for the weak. Your children will rank low in the Sept. You bring dishonor to our name."

"He's not a coward."

No, he wasn't, but he wouldn't deny the thought of letting someone inject him with drugs gave him the chills. Why the fuck should he trust these strangers with his life and health? Why should he take them at face value?

This is my body they're talking about using for experiments.

Supposedly, they could help him. What if they lied? What if they wanted to continue where Bittech started?

Don't trust.

Never trust.

Coward.

He couldn't be sure who spoke the word, and yet it hung with almost visible presence. Fuck. And this was why mostly men held the Darwin award titles.

Because we are fucking stupid, that's why. A sigh left him as he turned around. "What is this obsession you all have with kids?"

Adopting a pose his teacher had—minus the ruler—Xylia explained. "The lines that survived must be preserved. We lost too many lineages when the purge happened. We must ensure it doesn't happen again. But we do the bloodline little favor when we mix it with weak cowards." Her gaze didn't shy from meeting his, labeling him with her derision.

Hell no. He might be a giant fucking lizard, but he still had some goddamned pride. He stalked toward the aunt. "You know nothing about me. Nothing. I didn't ask to be like this. You have no idea what it's like to have to hide because your appearance causes screaming chaos." High-pitched shrieks that were funny to his cold side. "It's not cowardly to say no to strangers when it comes to drugs."

"Medicine."

"Still from a stranger. Would you let just anyone inject something into your body?"

"He's not completely stupid." The aunt addressed this to Aimi, ignoring him completely.

"You are unbelievably rude," he snapped.

"And you are overly emotional. Get a hold of yourself."

Get a hold of himself? She'd not gone through what he had. She didn't get it. Or understand that his life wasn't his own. He had someone relying on him. "I can't take any chances right now until I save my baby sister from Parker."

"Parker? Are we talking the Parker on the SHC?"

"Yes."

"And he has your sister?"

"He's been holding her against me for years, forcing my family and me to do his bidding."

"And you did not wage war upon him?" The aunt said it so matter-of-factly, as if it were a simple conclusion.

"We tried." Got punished. More than a few Mercers had left the bayou to serve time behind bars. Others hadn't left. They were just not seen again. It made a once strong family crumble. "We tried, and thought we had it when everything at Bittech went to hell. But we failed. We failed to get my sister. Failed to kill Parker, and now, he has outed us to the world."

"You mean he outed shifters. Not much of a loss. They will pave the way. At least the humans know nothing of our kind yet. And given how they've reacted, we may never tell them dragons walk among them." The aunt pursed her lips in disapproval.

Another one who believed they were something impossible. "Okay. I see the delusion moonbeam suffers from is a family thing. Dragons. Really? You don't seriously think anyone will believe that." He couldn't stop a snicker.

Xylia blinked and for a moment seemed at a loss for words. "You don't believe in dragons."

"Not for a second. I've seen all kinds of shifters in my life. Big and small. Hairy, feathered, and scaled. No one, and I mean *no one*, has ever said anything about dragons." His eyes widened as he had a sudden thought. "Unless you're Komodo dragons. I saw some once at the zoo. The non-sentient variety, of course. They are pretty cool, even if they are just a fancier kind of gator."

Shock rounded Xylia's mouth. "Did your mate just imply we're lizards?"

Aimi winced. "Yes. But in his defense, he truly seems to not know about our kind."

"But he's a dragon. I can smell it."

"I know. I've tried telling him, but he insists otherwise." Aimi shrugged. "Perhaps the experiments at Bittech addled his memories."

"Or perhaps I am telling you the truth," Brandon interjected.

"And what is the truth?" asked the aunt.

"I'm just a gator from the Everglades who had some gene splicing done, resulting in this." He fanned his hand down his body. "This isn't a hybrid shape as you keep calling it. This is me. And only me. Ain't no drug gonna fix it."

"Scientists changed your genetics, you say?"

"Yes."

He didn't move as Xylia approached and sniffed him. Scent was huge among shifters. Humans tended to be visual, deciphering things with their sight, but with shifters, and animals more specifically, the nose could paint an even more vivid picture. The nose didn't lie, usually.

The aunt took a step back, her brow creased and her gaze pensive. "He smells unlike anyone I've come across, but despite the oddity of it, I would stake a good portion of my hoard that he's dragon."

"Hoard? As in treasure? Way to perpetuate the myth."

"All dragons have a hoard," the aunt replied as she turned around and began to walk again.

"What's in this hoard? Treasure chests, gold coins, jewelry?"

"To a certain extent. I also collect vintage muscle cars and race horses." Xylia waved a hand overhead. "Zahra, her mother, she is obsessed with original *Star Wars* toys."

"And Aunt Yolanda collects pool boys," Aimi muttered, tossing him a saucy grin.

"What have we told you about gossip, young lady?"

"Make it juicy."

"I think you have me confused with your

Eve Langlais

Aunt Waida."

The constant verbal barrage proved fascinating, so much so he kind of just watched. He came back to the moment when Xylia addressed him. "This is my apothecary. Step inside."

"Why?"

"Again with the stupid questions." For a lady with an elegant appearance, she rolled her eyes like a champ. "Come in because I want to try something."

Brandon frowned. "Try what? I told you it can't be fixed."

"So you keep saying. Let me guess, a man told you that."

"Yes." This was fast becoming the second strangest conversation of his life, the first being Aimi's declaration that he was a dragon.

"Let me see if I understand. You took the word of your enemy? Because I assume you are not friends with the person who did this." She swept her hand at him.

"No, not friends."

"You let your enemy tell you it was irreversible, and you believed him. Did you get a second opinion?"

His lips tightened.

"Did you try any sort of treatment plan?"

He could almost feel the ghostly cuff of his mother with a muttered, "Idiot."

Her voice softened. "Let me help you, boy."

A hand gripped his forearm, and he didn't have to look down to know Aimi touched him. "You can trust her."

He wanted to say, "I don't even know if I trust you," but held the words inside because, oddly enough, he did trust her.

Ssshe tells the truth.

"It won't hurt."

"That's what the doctors said before the agony started." Along with the emasculating screams. Over time, even that pain failed to rouse him.

"Incompetent quacks. They try to work only modern science on what is, in many respects, ancient magic. I do a mix of the two."

"Do it, or I'll call you a chicken." Aimi clucked.

"Did you just double gator dare me?"

"More like triple, which means you can't say no now," Aimi replied, linking her arm through his and tugging him after her aunt. "What do you have to lose?"

His life? Not much of a loss, given it wasn't worth shit these days. What of his sister? He'd not even come close enough yet to doing anything to help her. He couldn't do anything, the whole lizard on two legs not being conducive for moving around in public.

Most of all, though...he wanted a chance to be normal again, and he wouldn't get that wish without taking some chances.

He took a step into the room. "Fine. Do your worst."

The aunt's lab reminded him of a medieval apothecary with dashes of modern convenience. Wooden shelves lined one of the walls and held hundreds of glass jars, each neatly labeled and barcoded. In contrast, another wall was all modern chrome and glass, the fridge and freezer combo holding yet more jars and vials, their contents backlit by a fluorescent light. In the middle of the room, a massive island took pride of place, split into several areas to work, the surfaces metal, granite, and more wood. On the third wall, at opposite ends, there were two archways. A peek inside showed one held an office with a massive desk and stacks of folders. The other room held beds and medical equipment, machines to read vital statistics, and other monitors that screamed hospital.

His bravado felt itself shrinking.

Leave. Now. His cold self didn't want to stay, but he could hardly run, not with Aimi watching and answers still forthcoming.

"How long have you been in this shape?" Xylia asked as she slid a finger over the jars, snaring some at random.

"Two years. Maybe a bit longer if you're counting from when treatment started and the changes began."

"Two?" He could tell he'd startled her. "And during that time, did you ever ascend into your dragon form or back into your human guise?"

Ascend into a dragon? Ha. He wished. "No. This is it. I have no other shape. Not anymore."

"No, this is the shape where you are stuck. Something in your psyche is obviously blocking you from fully transforming."

"Maybe because I'm not a dragon."

"Let's find out for sure, shall we?"

"You mean there's a test? Do I have to like breathe fire? Or eat a princess?" He shot a sly look at Aimi, who snickered.

"Yes, there's a test. Our race is an old one, and just like the shifters can differentiate their kind, so can we with a little help. The testing serum was developed in the Dark Ages by hunters who sought our treasures. They used to visit our courts in disguise, doing their best to oust us. We thought the formula destroyed until the Spanish Inquisition resurrected it. That was the last time it was used."

"Given you know how to make it, I'm going to guess you didn't destroy the recipe?" Despite himself, he found himself drawn into the imaginary narrative.

"Of course, we destroyed it. We wiped all traces of it from human annals and histories, but we kept the secret for ourselves. All knowledge is a treasure that should never be destroyed. We don't use it often, given we can obviously tell by scent who is dragon and who is not, yet given your odd story, let us perform a proper test that will tell us if you're dragon or not."

"How does it work? What do I have to do?"

"Donate some blood."

Before he could agree, Xylia poked him with a needle.

"Ouch." He glared at the aunt.

"Don't be a baby," Aimi chided.

"You could warn a guy when you're going to poke him with sharp objects."

"Is all your line so difficult?" was the reply as the aunt dropped his blood into a beaker. She added a few drops to it from a small vial that shone bright red. Sprinkled in a pinch of silvery powder. Added a purple sprig of something and then swirled the contents together.

It sizzled then foamed. It also changed rapidly into every color of the rainbow before settling on a dull green.

A part of him couldn't help but be disappointed. He might not believe in dragons, but for a moment, a part of him kind of hoped the test would say he was. "Guess I don't need to say I told you so."

Two sets of eyes perused him, and he could only ask, "What?" Why did they look at him with such shock? "Did I fail that badly?"

"On the contrary, you passed." The aunt looked pained as she added, "Your Grace."

Chapter Six

It couldn't be. They'd not seen one of his kind in centuries. Not since the purge. That line was thought to be dead. Wiped out.

And yet, there was no mistaking the color of the fluid.

"He's royalty?" she queried. "Are you sure?"

"We could run it again to be certain," said her aunt.

"And here comes the scam. You know," Brand said as he moved away from them, chastising with the shake of his head, "I might have been born on the wrong side of the bayou, and I might look like a dumb beast, but I am not a complete fucking moron. You're trying to pull one over on me. First trying to convince me that I'm a dragon and, now, supposed royalty. And even better, *long-lost* royalty." He made a sound of disgust. "You should have stuck to something more believable." He moved to the door, but Aimi stood in front of it.

"We are not fucking with you."

"Aimi! Language."

She couldn't help rolling her eyes. "Can you get your priorities straight? I am trying to stop him from killing me here, Auntie."

"I am not going to kill you." The words spat

forth, and their steely chill matched that in his eyes. "I might be a monster, but I'm not a murderer."

"I know you won't kill me. Dragons don't kill their mates."

"I'm not a fucking dragon!" he yelled.

"Language!" hollered Aimi's aunt.

"Fuck your language. I am not falling for this."

"Falling for what, the truth?"

"Bullshit."

"Not bullshit." For once, her aunt didn't say anything. Aimi held out her hands, a calming gesture, at least she hoped, given she had a pretty tall hybrid bulking himself and glaring. "You are a dragon. Or, at least, your genetics indicate you are."

"The test is wrong."

"That is possible." Aimi shrugged. "There are surely exceptions."

"Not really. It's never happened before," her aunt interjected.

"Well, it failed just now because I guarantee you, I am not a dragon. And even if by some messed-up fucking chance I am, no way am I descended from royalty."

"Are you sure you were not born like this?" Xylia paced around him.

"Like I told moonbeam, I'm a gator. Just a regular ol' swamp variety. It's the experiments that changed me and gave me wings and the look of a T-rex with longer arms."

"Even if the test failed, your scent also claims it."

"Wouldn't know. I can't smell myself." A weird shifter trait. They could scent others with ease, but when it came to their own scent, a pure blank spot.

"You claim experimentation, which given today's science could account for some mutations, but there must have been something there to trigger. Perhaps a recessive gene. What is your family name again?"

"Mercer."

Aunt Xylia shook her head. "Never heard of them."

"Surprising, given we're often in the news for misdemeanors." His lips quirked, and Aimi stifled a giggle at her aunt's face.

"Your family is criminal? Your mother won't like that, Aimi," Xylia said.

"Mother will find a way to spin it. By the time our first child is born, she'll have the Mercers portrayed as some kind of prevailing mob family and use the scandal of it to have fabulous parties."

"The fantasy world you live in is fascinating and, apparently, hereditary." His glance bounced between Aimi and her aunt.

"How does he keep denying what he is? How can one deny being a dragon? Were you dropped on your head as a child?" her aunt asked him.

"Probably. But the number of times still won't change the fact that I'm not a dragon, unless we're talking the one in my pants."

Aimi fired a fist to his gut for his impertinent reply and hit a wall. She managed to keep a stoic face.

"You can fly," Aimi pointed out.

"But I can't spit fire."

"Fire is overrated. So very uncontrollable. Why anyone would want to spit at anything instead of fighting claw to claw is beyond me." Xylia's lips twisted.

"She prefers the personal touch," Aimi confided. "According to Adi—"

"Who's Adi?"

"My sister. Anyhow, her theory is that my mother and aunts brawl in human shape to keep the laundry services in business. Auntie likes to wear white. It takes a special touch to get the blood out of silk."

He pinched his nose and closed his eyes. "Why are you telling me this? I mean, who admits to having a homicidal aunt?"

"Who said I killed anyone? Show me a body. Does someone need to disappear?" Xylia narrowed her gaze on Brand, and Aimi snapped her fingers.

"No threatening my mate, Auntie. He's my ticket out of here."

"I am not going anywhere with you, and I really think I shouldn't even be here."

"Don't start with the I'm-gonna-leave shit—"

"Aimi!"

"Fine, the I'm-gonna-leave fucking bullshit," she shouted with a roll of her eyes. His lips twitched as he tried not to laugh. "You want to know what you are. I'll tell you what are, and I don't even need a potion to do it." She stepped closer to him, close enough that she had to tilt her head to still see his face. "You are mine."

"You can't be serious about that." He turned away and to Xylia added, "Whatever you think I am, I'm not. And you can't allow her to bind herself to me. I am not a dragon."

"Have you seriously never pondered the fact

that dragons might exist? Heard a rumor?" Curiosity lilted her words.

"Never. Why?"

"Because your uncle, Parker, knows."

"I highly doubt that. If he knew, he would have blabbed."

"By all accounts, your uncle is wily, and is probably saving that information for a time he thinks it will benefit him." Aunt Xylia pointed to his wings. "If your uncle did this, then perhaps it was only possible because he knows something about your family. Do you have any unexplained bastards in your family? Were you perhaps born from an unwed mother or by an unknown father?"

"Have we gone from calling me 'Your Grace' to hoping I'm a bastard?" Brand had a tendency to deflect when things got uncomfortable.

"You are right about one thing. We know next to nothing about each other. Perhaps my previous address to your grace was premature."

"So now I'm not a dragon?" he asked.

"Yes, you are," Aimi hastened to interject. "And don't you even try to deny it, Auntie. You and I both know what that color means." Aimi pointed to the potion, the shade unmistakable. The colors were something they all learned at dragon school. Madame Drake's School of Manners not only provided lessons in being a proper snob—hold your head at an angle, use this fork first, no bodily noises in public— the school also provided a crash course for dragonlings to learn their history in a more fleshed-out manner than simply via family members who may have embellished certain key historical points.

"The potion is a shitty shade of green. Not

exactly exciting if you ask me."

"You're right. The color itself is less than exciting. It also has nothing in common with gold, just like the hue for our family test is a dull rusty color, quite atrocious, given our silver heritage. The yellows turn a very strange pink, while the seadrakes, who are blue for the most part, turn the solution clear."

"So, what color of dragon am I then according to this?" He pointed to the test tube. "Purple? Aquamarine? How about a very cool black with gray undertones?"

"It says you're a gold."

He peered down at his bared torso. "Gold? Really? You have seen me, right?"

Aunt Xylia examined his wings, but when she would have touched, he flinched away. It didn't stop her query. "You've never ascended, have you?"

"What's 'ascended?'"

"A stage most dragonlings pass in puberty. When you embrace your dragonself for the first time."

"Does it make a difference?" Aimi asked.

"Yes, because the color he wears now is that of a youngster, not a mature hybrid."

"So that's not his true color?" Aimi ran a finger down his chest, and he held still for it, muscles rigid, but he didn't move away.

"Usually, the dragonlings don't have the strength or ability to pull their hybrid, so I've never seen an un-ascended half-shift before. I would imagine, should he ascend to his true dragon, that his hybrid color will change, which, if the test can be believed, is gold."

He shook his head. "Except I can't change. This is it."

"Don't be a diva," Aimi remarked. "My aunt said she has something to try. What I'm more interested in finding out is if you're suitable as a mate. Is he?" In other words, could her mother object and block her plan for leaving the house?

Forget leaving. She'd better not try and keep me from my mate.

"Despite his lack of ascendance, he is more than suitable. Should he truly be gold, then joining with him will greatly benefit our Sept. And should your children be golden…" Her aunt smiled.

Then Aimi would have the biggest hoard. Fist pump. "He is my ticket out of here."

He latched on to those words. "You do realize I'm standing right here listening to you plotting to use me? Don't I get a say?"

"No."

Before his brow could furrow any further, Aimi tickled his chin. "Don't frown. This will be a good thing. A fun thing," she purred.

"I'm not looking for fun. I want to find my sister."

"Ah, yes, the sister. I'll have to get Adi working on that."

"You're going to help me?"

"Of course. Think of the return of your sister as my mating gift." It would also ensure Parker understood that messing with Brand and his family meant messing with the Silvergraces. There was a reason no one told stories about messing with the Silver Sept. Dead men kept their mouths shut.

"You're blackmailing me into marrying you,"

he stated, a hint of incredulity in his tone.

"Blackmail, bribery, they are better options than handcuffs and a shotgun." To this day, everyone mocked Waida's wedding picture.

"You're fucking nuts."

"Language."

To Aimi's surprise, he respected Xylia's admonishment. "You're fudging nuts. But tell you what, moonbeam, you help me get my sister back, and if your aunt can turn me back into a man, I'll marry you. Hell, if I can be me again, I'll even give you some of those babies you keep yammering on about."

The proposal—with benefits for them both—practically wet her panties. Sometimes a hoard grew with a simple promise. The best kind of treasure to own. "We have a deal." She turned from Brand to her aunt. "Fix him." Imperious demand at its best.

Mocking laughter in reply. "'Fix him,' she says. It might not be that easy." Xylia tapped her lower lip. "He is caught between the dragon and man. Both equally pulling. If I tip the balance one way, then the other may be forever lost."

"What do you mean forever lost? You mean if I became a man, I might never shift again?" His wings rustled.

"Or, if you ascend to your true dragon shape, you may perhaps never walk as a man again."

"At this point, I'd take being a man if given the choice."

"I might have something that will work, then." Her aunt went roaming the rows of shelves, running fingers along labels, plucking jars at random and returning them. She eventually found what she wanted on a high shelf tucked partially behind a wooden box inscribed with symbols. Setting it down, Xylia blew at it. The staff kept the jars well dusted, but given how Xylia struggled with the lid, whatever the container held, it had not been used in a while.

With a grunt and a word Aimi would have sworn was French for fuck, her aunt opened it. Holding out her palm, Xylia tipped the jar that appeared to hold a small handful of swirled black and white beads rolling around the bottom. "This should work. They had better work since I hate wasting one, given how hard these are to come by these days now that the mermaids no longer trade with those on land."

"Mermaids?"

He was so cute when his faced scrunched in skepticism. There was so much for Aimi to show him. Places to go and explore.

Together.

As in not alone.

Interesting…

The thought surprised her. She'd not expected to ever get married, and if she did, she assumed she'd continue living as she pleased with occasional conjugal visits. It was how her parents' marriage worked, and she knew of others who also treated it as a business arrangement. However, it didn't have to be that way.

Much as Aimi valued her independence, she had to admit that there were times she longed for the relationships she saw on television. Wanted a lover who made her smile and shared adventures with her. She knew a thing like that would never happen with the Harolds of this world, but then again, Harold and every other man she'd met didn't make her pulse race when they spoke.

Humans might find Brand monstrous, and perhaps he was to the humans, but Aimi saw an attractive male. She saw the strength in his shape, the will to survive against the odds. He was cunning; cunning enough that he'd found her without all the trimmings she had at her disposal. There was bravery there, too, under the cynicism and a noble core that she coveted.

He might have been born in mud, but that did not define him as a dragon.

True dragon majesty comes from within. Unless you had the biggest hoard, which trumped all.

Pinching it between two fingers, her aunt held up the bead. "These are the unfertilized offspring of the mermaids who do not manage to mate. They spawn an egg every decade, so as you can imagine, these are rare. And rarer still since the humans forced them to retreat to the deep that they might not find themselves hunted anymore. So many species the humans have destroyed. It took generations for the dragons to rebuild, bigger and stronger than before. Our time is soon coming."

His lip lifted in a sneer. "Now you sound like my uncle."

"Would it surprise you if I said, in many ways, your uncle is right?"

"You'd agree with a madman?"

"He makes some valid points," Xylia countered. "He is correct when he says we should not have to live in shadow. We should not fear being hunted into the ground by humans. Predators should rule the world, not the sheep."

A sentiment Aimi also shared, even if she never expressed it aloud. It surprised her to hear her aunt admitting it.

"And freaky comment of the day goes your aunt." Brand clapped and shook his head.

Aimi couldn't help but grin. "The day isn't quite over yet."

"There is much about this world you don't know, boy."

"Back to 'boy?' Damn, I am really missing being called Your Grace."

"If you want the title, then ascend. Until then, you're just another dragonling, subject to everyone's rules."

"I'm almost thirty."

"Still a baby." Xylia's lips quirked. "With so much to learn."

Aimi waved a hand to stop her aunt before she started. "I'll teach him our history later. We need to get moving on the rescue of his sister so that I might claim him. Should word get out that he's a possible royal, then the other Septs might try and snare him."

"Snare me for what?" He was adorably clueless.

"Breeding, of course. You are new blood, and if you truly are a gold, then everyone will want you."

"So I'm to expect a horde of women to kidnap me to have their wicked way?" He laughed, the sound deep with a hint of decadence. "Let them."

"Like hell," she snarled. "No one will be putting a hand on you, or they'll lose it.

"I won't need your protection, moonbeam, since no one is going to chase down a monster for sex."

"You don't need to have sex to extract sperm. You don't even need him conscious."

It wasn't just Brand who gaped at her aunt.

Xylia shrugged. "Just saying. And we're off topic. You wanted to change him back. He needs to eat this, followed by a glass full of..." Her words tapered as she opened a refrigerated unit and returned with a brown bottle. "Drink this."

"You want me to eat a pearl and chug what looks like piss?"

"Yes."

"Will this make me into even more of a mutant?"

"Possibly."

"Aunt Xylia!"

"Like I said before, it will tip him into either man or dragon, but given he's stubborn, I'm leaning toward man. At least temporarily."

"Will it hurt?"

"It is my job to heal things, not hurt them."

He held out his hand, and Xylia dropped the pearl in it. He then wrapped his fingers around the cold glass with the amber liquid. He hesitated. There might have been a clucking noise, and it may or may not have come from Aimi.

With a scowl, he popped the bead in his mouth and quickly chugged from the glass.

He slapped the empty bottle down and made a face. "That was revolting. With a fishy aftertaste."

"Castor oil."

"Castor oil helps the change?" Aimi asked.

"It's for his foul language. The pearl is what will fix him."

Brand crossed his arms. "Nothing is happening."

"Give it a moment. Men," her aunt huffed in Aimi's direction, "always so impatient. Especially in the bedroom. Always rushing to get to the main event."

"Still not wor—Argh. Ugh. Irk." The grunts contorted his features, and Brand dropped to his knees as his leathery skin rippled and his wings shuddered.

"What did you do?" he gasped. "You said it wouldn't hurt."

"Auntie lied." Aimi knelt by him. "The cures almost always hurt." Because they worked.

Knowing this, her aunt was ready with a powder that she blew into his face, whispering, "Sleep."

Chapter Seven

The collar burned at his neck, and he lay shuddering on the floor, his body a trembling mess. Once again, he'd fought what his jailers wanted of him. Once again, they'd tortured him until he could take no more.

But at least when he was limp, he couldn't do as they asked. Some evil even he couldn't be forced to commit. His strength of will didn't pass itself on to others, and he had to hear the screams and the grunts and wish he could die.

Because the pain was never-ending, the horror always beginning anew, starting in the morning when he looked in the mirror and saw a monster.

A monster who deserved the pain.

No more pain.

A beast who acted upon baser instincts.

Because you had no choice.

A guy who was going to snap if… "Get out of my head!"

"Morning to you, too, sunshine." This time, she spoke to him aloud.

"What the fuck did you do to me?" A vehemence he found hard to maintain, given he didn't seem to suffer from any pain and he found himself comfortable. Very comfortable. The mattress he lay on had just enough cushion to cradle him. The sheets smelled of vanilla—and woman, mustn't forget that candy-like scent of woman that made him think of moonbeams. The fabric felt silky soft against his skin, but even better was the naked body snuggled against his.

Back up a second. Naked body pressed against his skin. *My skin.*

Holy shit!

Without a thought for the woman cuddling him, Brandon dove out of the bed and stood on two feet—not claws—and slapped himself, his flesh pale and, yet, human. Not scaled.

"I'm me." He whispered the word, barely daring to believe it. But did it extend everywhere? A glance between his legs showed his mighty snake hanging like he remembered, along with his balls. What of his face?

Fingers palpated his features, and they felt right, but he needed to see. "A mirror. I need a mirror," he muttered as he turned around, finally spotting one over a dresser. He didn't need to get close to see his reflection, a reflection that now seemed strange after so long. Even his hair stuck out in long strands.

"It worked. It actually fucking worked."

"Of course, it did. I told you my Aunt Xylia knew her stuff. Now, if Aunt Waida had managed to pour something in you, then that might have been a different thing. You could have ended up with horns or a second cock."

He whirled. "Thank you."

"For not growing a second cock? I don't know. That could have been interesting if you ask me."

"Don't screw with me, moonbeam. Thank you for this. For drawing me here and having your aunt cure me."

Her lips quirked. "If you want to thank me, then why don't you come here." She patted the mattress beside her.

It was tempting. Everything about Aimi was tempting, from her violet sloe eyes to her shimmering waves of hair. As for her body, she didn't try to hide it, letting the blanket only partially cover it. The alabaster beauty of her limbs beckoned. He wanted to go over there and lick every inch of her. It was a struggle to declare, "I can't." Not because he didn't want to.

Hard to hide the evidence of his interest when his gaze dropped. The fact that she stared didn't help. He swelled larger. "According to that, you can, and should, join me." She patted the mattress again.

He tried to ignore the fact that he sported an impressive erection, an erection that wanted nothing more than to sink inside this wondrous woman. A woman he barely knew. A crazy lady who thought dragons were real. A woman who'd given him hope.

Hope and a chance he couldn't squander.

"A part of me really wants to stay." He eyed the curve of her breast peeking past the edge of the sheet; the leg, with its shapely calf, and the partially revealed thigh; a thigh that if spread wider would give him a peek of pink. He averted his gaze. "But now that I'm normal again, I owe it to my sister to rescue her."

"And we will rescue her. Soon. Very soon. But until the arrangements are finalized, we need sleep." She patted the bed, and the smile held so much invitation.

The temptation was almost too much.

"Sleeping with you wasn't the deal."

"But we'd both have so much fun." Her lower lip jutted in a pout that practically ordered him to suckle.

I could kiss her if I wanted to. I have lips again. Now there was something he'd not indulged in for a long time. Hell, he'd not indulged in any kind of fun with a woman since the change. So why exactly was he saying no?

It was not as if he could go anywhere at the moment. He had no clothes, no money or identification, and without his wings, how would he travel?

He wasn't even sure what time of day or what day it was. The curtains were drawn, and the room almost pitch-black. Only the faintest of illumination came from a doorway that he would wager good money was a bathroom.

A bathroom meant a shower. *Fuck me*, when was the last time he'd had one of those?

In a blink, he stood in the large glass enclosure. He might have groaned when the hot spray hit his skin. Moaned, too.

"Did I seriously just get dumped for a shower?" She sounded amused.

Turning his head, he squinted at Aimi through one eye, his long, wet lashes fighting to cling. His hands were braced on the wall, and he leaned slightly forward, letting the hot needles of water hit his head then roll down his back. The clear glass barrier between them perhaps prevented droplets from spraying, but they didn't hide him from her or her from him.

He stared. He couldn't help himself. In bed, she'd proven alluring, showcasing only parts of her trim figure. He'd managed to resist, having enough self-control to not be swayed by mere arms and legs exposed.

But she didn't wear a sheet now. Nor pajamas or clothes of any kind. Aimi stood without an ounce of shyness, shoulders back, breasts a bare handful and peaked with fat nipples. Her waist had only the slightest of indents flaring into slim hips. Her mound sported silvery curls that matched the hair on top.

Purrrrrfect. Again, he almost hummed because of her.

"Get a good hard look and weep because this is what you abandoned for a shower."

A shower that left him finally feeling clean, and in the mood to get dirty. "It's a big shower. Room enough for two." The flirting he used to indulge in came easily to his lips, and he crooked a beckoning finger.

Her hair rippled as her chin angled. "I'm not dirty."

For some reason that made his lips quirk, and he turned fully to face her before settling back until his shoulders hit the wall, one leg bent and resting on it. "I am." He looked down and then back at her.

It was brazen, and he expected a blush, an indignant reply, even laughter, although he hoped she'd just join him. What he didn't expect was…

"Well, at least he's not impotent. We'll have your aunt test the viability of his swimmers later."

Test the what of the what?

Brandon straightened and dropped his hands to cover himself as a woman he'd not yet met entered the bathroom behind Aimi. The resemblance was startling so he wasn't surprised to hear Aimi gasp, "Mother. What are you doing in here?"

"Apparently, my daughter claims a male, and I am the last to know and meet him."

"I haven't claimed him yet."

"Of course, you haven't, because you are always leaving things to the last minute."

"We just met. Surely we're allowed a few minutes before we bind ourselves for life."

"Perhaps I should have given you a few minutes. Maybe then all the blood would be in your head instead."

"Can you blame me? The man is pretty."

Pretty? Brandon was many things, but he wouldn't have said that.

Eyes perused him with a clinical detachment that weighed him, judged him, and shriveled his balls. "He's doable."

"Mother!" said in shock. To him, Aimi mouthed, "She has no boundaries."

"I am your mother. Those don't apply to me. And before you ask, I always know when you are sassing. You should know that by now. Tell your beau to get dressed at once that you might introduce him to me and explain what in the thirteen colors is going on." Aimi's mother barked her wishes, but Brandon was used to bullying tactics.

She wanted him dressed. Fuck that. Brand straightened and pushed away from the wall. He stepped out of the shower, dripping wet, ignored the towel hanging there, and walked right over to Aimi's mom. He stood over her, forcing her to look up or stare at his chest.

As soon as their gazes met, he smiled, wickedly. His tone danced with mirth as he said, "You must be Aimi's ma."

"I am Zahra Silvergrace, Contessa of the Silver Sept, and matriarch of the Silvergrace family."

"Nice to meet you. How's about a hug?" The arms he wrapped around her were very wet, as was the rest of him, and she wore silk.

It was worth the screech from Zahra to hear Aimi's silver-belled laughter.

What he liked less was the older woman putting him flat on his ass in a series of lightning-quick moves and pinning him with a heel. With slitted eyes spitting green, she stated, "If you weren't already almost mated to my daughter—"

"You'd marry him off to someone else in the family. We both know you wouldn't let your dignity kill a mateable male." Aimi pushed at her mother. "Now get off him."

Zahra glared. "He started it."

"And you totally deserved it. Barging in here like this. You wouldn't have done that to Eugenia's son."

"Eugenia's son wouldn't have been trying to entice you to shower with him."

"I wanted to do more than shower," he felt a need to interject.

Aimi held back her mother, who growled, "Don't make me school you again."

"Try it. But maybe next time, I'll forget you're a girl." Actually, the very fact that Zahra was a woman and Aimi's mom meant he'd have to take any beating she meted out. Anything less meant shredding his mancard.

"You think you can take me, gutter creature?"

"That's swamp. And possibly illegitimate, too. We never did find a marriage license for my folks." He rose from the floor and finally decided to wrap a towel around his loins, lest Zahra react like a cat and go after the dangling bits.

"He's a bastard? You're bringing a bastard into the fold?" Her mother looked quite appalled.

"But he's gold."

Aimi's mother eyed him in the cold, calculating way he'd seen before in his Aunt Tanya's eyes when she measured up something to put in the pot. It made the other churchgoers nervous.

"A possible gold. Who is un-ascended and related to that idiot, Parker. What on earth makes you think I'd approve of this."

"Because you and I both know I've run out of choices. Besides, just imagine if he does ascend. No other Sept can claim a gold for breeding."

Everywhere he went, folks wanted to use him. Funny how Aimi's need to use him as a mate and father didn't bother him, though. Rather it filled him with a warm, possessive feeling. Still, he couldn't just let her talk about him as if he were an object. "Your mercenary side is coming out again, moonbeam," he chided.

The mother replied. "Thank you. I did my best to raise her right. But flattery won't change my mind. I don't think you're acceptable. Not yet."

"Too late for that, Mother. He's mine."

"If that's true, then why haven't you marked him?"

"Because we made a bargain." Aimi's face made a moue. "He wants his sister present for the ceremony."

"More swamp people in our home? Perhaps you'd like them to pitch tents on the lawn?"

"Golly, maybe we'll string up some clotheslines and do our laundry in that big ol' fountain out front." Brandon adopted his best yokel voice, which didn't endear him to dear old mom.

"I see someone requires some castor oil."

"Aunt Xylia gave him some already."

"Obviously not enough."

"He chugged the whole bottle."

"And that right there should tell you he isn't one of us." The mother spun on her heel. "A true dragon can't stand the taste."

"Daddy used to gargle it," Aimi said, practically singing the claim.

"Argh." The mother stomped out of the room with an inarticulate cry.

"Well, that went well."

She shrugged. "It could have been worse. You're still alive."

"And you're still naked."

She looked down. "I am." Her lips quirked. "Are you still dirty?"

Yes, as a matter of fact, he was. He drew her close, reveling in the feel of her against him. Silky-soft skin. Even softer hair.

For the past two years, he'd thought getting this close to a woman—who wouldn't scream and struggle—would be impossible. Who wanted to touch a monster?

But he wasn't a monster anymore.

Don't be so sure. I'm still here, the cold part of him reminded, finally speaking for the first time since his waking.

His other half, the mutated part of him, still existed, but he was in control.

As if needing to assert his tenuous grasp on his humanity, he cupped the back of her head and drew her on tiptoe, close enough that he could press his mouth to hers.

The madness of the act didn't escape him. Aimi used him. For what purpose exactly he wasn't sure. Perhaps she truly did want him as mate and father of her babes, but there was more to it than that.

Her lips, soft and pliant under his, her lithe body pressing, he really didn't give a damn what that reason was. It was enough to feel again.

To touch.

To taste.

To tumble her on a bed—not a rooftop or a grassy glade. Enough to have her greedy hands clutching at him, the sharp edges of her nails digging into his flesh as she drew him close and sucked at his mouth then his tongue.

The hardness of his erection pressed against her, the towel but a barrier, a thin one easily removed. He shifted, tugging the damp terry cloth away from skin, letting the head of him nudge at her.

He was impatient. He knew he was impatient. He had to slow down. But how could he?

What if the curse returned? What if this was the one and only chance he ever got?

Then I'd better make it good.

He shifted to the side enough that his body

held his weight on the bed, and he could free a hand to skim the planes of her flesh, stroking over her ribs, over her flat tummy. He dragged his fingers through the silky curls of her mound.

The rosy tips of her breasts beckoned, and he clasped one with his lips, sucking greedily at the tip, unable to stop himself from humming in pleasure, especially when she clasped his head and pulled him closer, uttering a breathy, "Yes."

Yes, indeed.

His fingers slid between her thighs and stroked at her velvety moistness. Her sex quivered at his touch, soaking his fingers in her honey.

It wasn't just bears that liked a lick.

Claim the treasure. The warm suggestion had him shifting, moving to a spot between her legs, draping her thighs over his shoulders, exposing her pink perfection.

At his first lap, she arched. At the second, she sighed. By the time he was busy flicking his tongue over the swollen nub of her clitoris, her head was thrashing. Her body wanted to buck, but he held it firmly, his hands keeping her steady that he might enjoy the treat.

He'd been mistaken when he called her honey. The taste of her was more than that. It drugged his senses, arousing him in a way he'd never imagined. He also felt connected to her, and thus wasn't surprised when amidst the soft pants and moans, he heard her thoughts,

More. Yes. Right there. Lick me.

Not exactly a conversation but still the most wondrous thing he'd ever heard.

It spurred him on, making his actions more

frenzied.

That's it. Now finger fuck me while you lick.

Like this? He rammed two fingers into her warm sheath, and she let out a cry.

Yes.

Her hips undulated against his hand as he lapped at her button. Her soft flesh pulsed around him, and he could feel her coiling, her pleasure tightening in a web around them both.

He let his lips travel up her flat stomach to her breasts, but only when he reached her lips did he slide a third finger into her.

Her sex tightened around him, and she gasped into his mouth. He pounded her and didn't have to wonder if she enjoyed it. He didn't just feel it on his fingers; he *felt it.* Felt it through her. The enjoyment, the excitement.

And when she came, it was so beautiful, so fucking erotic, it slammed into him, and as she climaxed around his fingers, so did he climax on the sheets, his cock unable to resist the excitement after so long.

An excitement he might have enjoyed more if someone hadn't said, "About time you were done," just before they shot him in the ass!

Chapter Eight

"Adi!" Aimi yelled her sister's name as she struggled out from the sudden dead weight of her almost mate. Almost mate because, once again her family—demon-spawned evil—pussy blocked her. It made her want to punch someone in the boob—and she really didn't give a damn if it was ladylike or not. It was her Aunt Waida who had taught her.

"People make the mistake of thinking a kick to the crotch will drop a chick as if it were the same as a blow to the balls on a man. Wrong. You give her a good shot right to the tit"—demonstrated in the bar with a rapid jab that sent a patron screeching to the floor—"and you will own that fight."

"Isn't that dirty?" she'd asked. Aunt Waida had smiled, and the scary part of the smile was that there was nothing cold or calculating about it. Aunt Waida looked genuinely happy as she'd said, "Yes. Yes, it is."

"If you're done playing hide the wiener, then get dressed. Mom wants to see you."

"Then she could have called or texted. While you could have tried something, like say, knocking. You didn't have to drug him." Which was better than having killed him.

Aimi wouldn't put it past her mother,

especially now that her matriarch realized he hadn't emerged from exactly pristine stock. The irony of it was that their family hadn't always been so hoity-toity and above reproach. More than one great-great-great-something had skirted the laws. Calling it the facilitation of dispensing goods was just a fancy name for smuggling.

Having heaved Brand's body to the side, Aimi noted he slumbered, and deeply at that, his mind a dark hole of nothing, whereas only moments before, it had been full of wonder and delight— *wonder and delight for me.*

This bond thing between them was proving kind of cool, at least during sex. The rest of the time…that remained to be seen. The idea of being that closely connected to anyone didn't exactly leave her feeling overjoyed. Her idea of marriage was meeting for the occasional bump and grind, sharing a bed when that happened, but otherwise, leading her own life. It was what her parents did, and it worked well for them.

But they mated because of a family merger. From the first moment I met Brandon, I felt something for him. And it defied all reason.

"Would you stop your whining? At least I let him finish you off before I zapped that sweet ass of his."

"Don't look at his ass." With a frown, Aimi drew a blanket over him. Her sister showed a little too much interest in his naked flesh. *My flesh.* And while the family shared many things, men weren't one of them—and BOBs were off-limits, too. When it came to the last piece of cake in the fridge, though? Game on.

"Kind of hard to miss seeing his ass, given he was humping your hip like crazy. And is it me, or did someone shoot early? You poor thing." Adi shook her head.

Aimi, however, saw things differently. "He did come just from giving me pleasure. Talk about super sexy and hot, not to mention flattering, knowing he finds me that desirable. Maybe you'll find someone someday who thinks you're the bomb." Aimi flicked her sister with her pastel punk look a glance. "Or not."

The jab worked. Adi crossed her arms. "I don't need a man to make me happy."

"Then I guess you don't want to know that he made me come harder with his fingers and tongue than anyone has ever managed. And that includes BOB. I can't wait to take a spin on his dick." Crude, but between her and her sister, there were no holds barred and no boundaries.

"Look at you, all pussy whipped already."

Aimi smirked. "Yes, I am. Jealous?"

"No," said in a vehement sulk. "While you were busy fucking around, some of us were working."

"Having a relationship is work, too. All that kissing and groping and…you know. Oh, wait, you don't know on account I found a man and you didn't." Yes, she did crown that taunt with a tongue poke. Some things a girl never grew out of, like harassing her twin—and watching Bugs Bunny. Except she kept hoping one day that unlucky coyote would catch the bird and eat it.

"You might have found a man, but that doesn't mean you'll get to keep him. Did you know he's from a family of swamp gators?"

She would keep him because he was hers. "I already know about his roots. He told me." And oddly enough, despite being raised to be a snob, she really didn't care. *He's the one I want.*

"You're not bothered by it?" Adi asked, an odd question coming from her, given she always seemed determined to do the opposite of what the family wanted. If their mother said behave, Adi played the hoyden. If a boy appeared to belong to the wrong side of the tracks, Adi jumped his bones. That rebellious streak drove their mother nuts—and meant Aimi often came across as the good daughter.

Until now. The question her sister posed was a good one. Did his roots bother her? Her mother had raised her to value her bloodline. From a young age, Aimi knew that she had a responsibility to pass on that bloodline by any means necessary. She hoped to do that with Brandon, but he wasn't a true-born dragon. He came from shifter stock, and not just shifter but of a caste considered low on the totem of power. *But lineage isn't everything.* Character and integrity and true inner strength were sometimes more important.

Fingers stroked over his forehead, brushing the strands of hair layered across it, and her soft reply was, "I don't care one bit." And that was the truth.

What bothered her more than Brand's genes was the fact that her mother, and probably a few other family members—because they did so love to meddle—wanted to discuss his existence, and probably his future. *Discussions*—said in mental quotes—meant arguing, in this case, arguing her case to keep Brand.

So be it. Aimi girded herself to defend him and her plans for him. On the subject of their mating, she would not budge. Since she didn't think her mother would take her seriously if she marched in there naked, she took a moment to pull on sweatpants and a shirt—designer brand, of course.

The several minutes it took to thread the maze of the house to her mother's office gave her time to formulate some arguments. She ignored the salutations of others, lost in her imagined rebuttals with her mother. She had no doubt they would argue. They always did. As the last of her mother's brood, and born years after her other sisters besides Ari and one brother, it meant her mom had way too much time to poke her nose in her affairs.

That would change once Aimi mated and moved out.

Entering the office—a place that even now brought her shoulders back and her hands smoothing the fabric of her shirt—she noted the meeting was a small one, consisting only of Aimi, her mother, and her Aunt Xylia.

"Where's everyone else?"

"We thought it best to keep some of the information about our guest to ourselves for the moment until we had a firm plan."

"Exactly how do you plan to keep it under wraps? It isn't as if he arrived in secret, and it's kind of hard to ignore the fact that I've got a big dude in my bed."

"Which is totally inappropriate, by the way." Disapproval pulled her mother's lips down. "You should have left him in Xylia's lab."

"Let's get one thing clear right now. He

belongs to me." Her eyes narrowed as she stated it. "Until we are properly mated, I will not be leaving him anywhere someone can get their grubby claws on him." Which she'd stupidly delayed with her promise to him.

Lips pursed, her mother cast a disapproving glare. Not the first time Aimi had gotten *the look,* so she let it roll off her back. "And this is why we are conducting this meeting quietly. Your strange obsession with this man isn't something I want broadcasted. For the moment, we've provided only the barest of cover stories to the family. The less they and the staff can blab about the *thing* you found, the better. We don't need any unwanted visitors."

In other words, they needed to guard against another Sept stealing Brand because of what he might be. Paranoia was their prime motivator after avarice. A dragon's motto, woven into more than one tapestry was, *See it, take it.*

Aimi's mother was right to be paranoid. Chances were their enemies spied, and if they suspected what the Silvergraces might have—a gold!—then the family's defense system could get a good workout.

Adi would be pleased. She'd spent months fine-tuning the safeguards to the mansion and grounds, and kept complaining she needed someone to give it a good run to test it. Brand proved that it still needed tweaking, given how close he'd made it to the main house before the drones deployed.

Her mother, dressed in an ivory pantsuit, paced behind her desk. Even at the ripe age of eighty—she'd had Aimi and Adi late in life—she didn't look a day over fifty, and a good fifty at that.

"What are we going to do about the thing? Did you leave him secured?"

"Do you mean Brand?" Aimi wasn't about to let her mother start things off discussing Brand as an object instead of a person. Even better than him being a person, he was a dragon—more or less. "I already told you, I left him sleeping in my bed."

"Is that really appropriate? You aren't yet mated, and we don't know enough about him. You trust much too easily."

Not usually, she didn't, but in his case, something told her she had nothing to fear. Then again, she'd never let something so paltry as fear get in her way. She was dragon. She feared nothing—but her Aunt Waida's cure for a hangover. Vile stuff. "Brand won't harm me."

"It's not you I'm worried about but your younger cousins. What if he was sent here to infiltrate and attack from within?"

"I think you need to put on some aluminum foil panties."

"You joke, but I am very serious. You don't know this man, and yet you have him in your room instead of secured in a cell."

"Don't you even think of putting him in the dungeon." Because all dragon castles had one, a throwback to the old days. "Brand is not our enemy, and he's perfectly safe in my room." She'd locked her door with a handprint. Only she, and her annoying sister with the same imprint, could open it—unless someone used a bazooka, and if that happened, she'd have bigger problems.

"At least you don't have him wandering the halls. Probably the first smart thing you've done since leading him to our home."

"I didn't lead him here. He came looking for me."

"I think you need to explain things from the beginning."

Aimi did, detailing their meeting for her mother. Never mind she'd already told Adi and Xylia. Her mother wasn't one to rely on second-hand information.

"He was sitting on a rooftop, and you didn't think to question why?"

"Um, no?" She shrugged.

"What if he was a spy for another Sept? Or an assassin? We have enemies you know."

"I know, but I think you're missing the bigger picture here. I found a male dragon, and not just any dragon. One with the potential to tip the balance of power." Nothing like dangling a carrot of prestige in front of her mother to have her start viewing him in a different light. *He'll make a nice addition to our hoard. My hoard.* But still, any advantage one Silvergrace acquired affected them all.

"Ah, yes, his potential," her mother said. "An impossibility more like. How can this be? A gold, after all this time? Could this be our enemies trying to fool us? Is this part of some grander plot?" She resumed pacing behind her desk. An impressive desk Aimi should add, carved from redwood, the beautiful natural swirls of worlds gleaming as the artist used the unique whorls and patterns to create a piece of art.

"Somehow, I doubt our enemies want us to have him. I think it's more likely he's exactly as he seems to be. Someone who escaped captivity." And was, even now, being hunted.

While Brand slept, Adi had kept her apprised of her investigation via text messages, and one of them said she had located more than one offer to bring Brandon in—alive. She also discovered he wasn't married, had no kids, and until his disappearance, had lived at home with his mother. But Aimi didn't let that bother her, given she also lived at home. For now…

Xylia lifted a stack of documents. "While tests indicate he is a possible gold, we have to remember that by his claims, he wasn't born that way."

"He came from the Bittech lab," her mother stated, more musingly than to inform.

No hiding that from her mother, even if Adi hadn't snitched. Her mother had her own information network.

According to the data gathered, Brandon's claims were true. While Bittech never truly divulged the nature of their projects, they never denied Brandon was a result; a result who went missing after the Great Reveal, according to reports.

"I don't know how they did it, but somehow, the scientists in that lab managed to turn him into a dragon."

"A possible dragon," Xylia corrected. "It could be that, due to the method of his becoming dragon, he will never ascend. Or have you so soon forgotten his issues with his hybrid shape?"

"Based on that alone, we should be worried. What did that imbecile Parker do? Exactly what was the purpose of his experiments? It seems we should have paid closer attention. Then again, what he did should have been impossible. Dragons can't be made." Anger creased her mother's features. "It's unnatural."

"It might be unnatural, and yet, according to all tests so far, he is dragon." Aimi stressed that point.

The tests proved it over and over, even the ones conducted while his body fought whatever battle it needed to return to a more natural state. The muscles in his body rippled, his skin undulated, grimaces tugged at his features. The struggle was real and intense.

The wait to see what Brand truly looked like did not go unnoticed by her aunt. She had teased: *"He's probably ugly. But at least he's well endowed."*

That was something they couldn't miss seeing. Stripping him to ease the transition of his body meant getting an eyeful. Better her than someone else. Bad enough her aunt got a peek.

Turned out, Brand was mighty fine. Better than fine, with thick, dark hair, and sharp features with a square and stubborn chin.

He'd lost no bulk in transition. A big hybrid turned into a big man. Big all over with pale skin and almost no hair on his body, even around his...

Not usually a shy girl, Aimi had looked away before her aunt could catch her and tease her even more.

Given his all-over girth, she could only wonder what kind of dragon Brand would make when he ascended.

The arguing of her mother and aunt brought her back to the present in the office, which had angry voices and not a yummy, naked Brand.

"I've run the test numerous times, and even

tested it against the blood of other dragons we keep in the freezers. It's always the same. It says he's gold."

"Impossible. Gold is extinct." Aimi's mother faced away from them, staring out her window over the lush gardens lit by a waning afternoon sun.

"How can you be sure they died out? I mean, look at us; we didn't. The silvers recovered from the purge, as did Septs scattered around the world." Aimi knew her history.

"Yes, many Septs and families did survive, but we had one thing in common: we knew of each other's existence. Knew and aided each other in surviving. No one has heard of the gold since those dark times."

"That's not entirely true," Xylia said, interrupting. "You know there were rumors."

"Are we peasants now to put stock in gossip?" her mother snapped.

But Aimi saw it for what it was, a denial. "What were the rumors?" She wondered if they were the same ones whispered at her finishing school.

Her mother rolled her eyes. "Isn't it kind of obvious? The rumors say that at least one gold survived, and because of some two-bit religious group, it keeps being circulated, even though there is no proof. None at all."

Xylia nodded. "Faith requires no proof. Sometimes, word of mouth is enough, and after the Septs had begun to find each other again after the purge, everyone seemed to have heard it—that the last gold queen had produced an egg with the king before she died."

"An egg?" Aimi's nose wrinkled. It caused no

end of discomfort to be reminded that, in the past, they'd chosen to hatch their young rather than carry them in their tummies.

"Do not disparage your roots. Back then, the human guise was the one rarely used. We were dragon, and we were proud. So proud." The nostalgic tone brought to mind stories told to Aimi when a youngling, stories of dragons owning the skies and flying in sunshine. Daylight flying was considered such a no-no now. Even nighttime flying was to be done only under guarded circumstances. There was a reason the property they owned resided so far out of town and encompassed so much land. It gave them a little spot to at least be themselves. A spot where there used to be no eyes watching, but now, with the advent of technology—curse you, satellites in the sky—even that was being taken from them.

If we cannot be dragon, then why are we holding on to the past? The glory days are over. We are bound by humanity and fear. A fear they'll come for us again.

Look at the Cryptozoids. They'd announced their presence, they'd told the world, "Here I am." The price of silver had gone through the roof, and the economy was booming—in the weapons sector. As smart business people, the dragons held more than a few stakes in those companies but also found a boom happened in home protection.

The Bite Back System will protect against unwanted hairy pests. Even the big ones. And it could be yours for only six installments of ninety-nine dollars.

What a waste of money. Everyone knew the Cryptos preferred hunting to breaking and entering. Dragons used to rule at the chase. Now, they flew on a roster so everyone got their fair share of airtime. It sucked. Big time.

The merits of coming out kept stacking. Perhaps it wouldn't be so bad? People loved dragons. Look how the watchers of a certain HBO drama reacted when a blonde queen took to the skies on the back of a winged avenger. Yes, she would admit to a certain guilty pleasure in watching *Game of Thrones*.

But the infamous GoT series never had to deal with the reality of how an egg was created. Certain conditions had to be met. None of them in human form.

"I still can't believe they, um, did the"—she wiggled her brows, unable to think of a delicate way to say fucking without getting in trouble—"you know, as dragons."

"Don't be such a prude. It's a natural part of dragon life."

"Used to be, Mom. When was the last time we had an egg hatch? I don't know of any cases. Do you?"

Her mother's lips pursed. "That is an indelicate thing to ask. What I will say is, yes, it does still happen. There is nothing obscene or wrong with fornicating in our true form."

"And," Xylia interjected, "there are benefits."

True. Instead of having a nine-month pregnancy, when a dragoness went into her reproduction phase, she could produce a few eggs. Once fertilized, the eggs could be stored, and wouldn't hatch until the right conditions were met. A lack of heir being the most common condition.

"So the queen supposedly plopped an egg centuries ago. Do we know if it hatched?" Aimi asked.

"No one knows. The rumors only say the queen hid an egg. A fertilized gold, and it's never been found."

It sounded like something out of a fable. "I call bullshit."

"Language!"

"Forget the language. I am a little pissed that I'm only finding out about this legend of a gold egg now."

"It's not a legend."

"It's like the difference between potato and *potahto.*" Aimi looked between her aunt and mother. "Which makes me wonder. You've known of this rumor for a long time obviously. Do you believe it?" Aimi wasn't sure she did. None of the histories ever spoke of an egg. In all of them, the golds had been decimated after leading a last-ditch attack against the humans. It failed.

"It doesn't matter if I believe it. It only takes a few to fuel a religion."

"This is the second time you've mentioned a religion. Dragons don't follow gods or doctrine. We have the Sept laws." The dumping of information began to grate. How many secrets did her mother hide?

"It's not a very big religion, not anymore, but it has existed since the purge. The believers worship the last golden mother and the last egg she birthed. Their story tells how she hid it, and that when the golden heir returns, he shall lead the dragons into the sun again."

"And now there's a hero to go with the fable." She rolled her eyes. "Do I even know who I am anymore? Why am I suddenly finding out about all this weird shit now?"

"Because, as you so eloquently put it, shit is happening now. Until recently, it was easy to mock and ignore the unwavering belief of a hidden religious sect. Like I said, they're small in number, and even more insane than those Templars. I mocked them when my mother finally revealed their presence to me. However, we seem to live in interesting times, and that belief is now stronger than ever."

"Why, though?" Aimi struggled to understand why people would cling to a vague rumor of an egg. Really, an egg? Even if it hatched after all this time, what could one dragon do? "Why believe in something so silly?"

"Is it silly?" Her mother fixed her with a stare and sighed. "Do you really have to ask why they want to believe? Use your head for something other than a perch for a crown."

"Give the child a break. She's had less time with the other Septs than we have. A lot of them are closing ranks, and we're not any different. We haven't taken in a foster dragonling in over a decade now. The advancement of technology has made all the Septs more careful."

"You mean more paranoid. As the dark times creep again, they look for the gold to save them," her mother muttered.

"What the heck is that supposed to mean?"

"The quote refers to a tenet of their belief. Now, like then, it was a dark time for dragons. No flying, no being who we are. Always hiding. We tried fighting back at first, but there were too many humans, and they had bows and spears, not to mention numbers. We started to die and quickly realized we wouldn't survive, not when we reproduced so slowly. We didn't have help from science back then. It left only one option."

Dragonkind had to hide, and the golden king, the last king, ordered his people to go and covered their retreat. But the goldens couldn't hide. As the most prized of the dragons, they were hunted hardest. They were decimated, especially since the golds, in their pride, refused to hide. Golds were fighters to the end, and it led to the end of their line.

Humans found and struck down the once proud ruling family, to the very last one. So many lost hope.

Her aunt was the one recounting the history, but giving it a twist Aimi never imagined. "Dragons had lost all hope. We wanted to fight, and yet we cowered in our caves. Lamenting our glory, mourning those fallen. It seemed like all was lost, and then the rumor emerged of a single egg, hidden away from the hunters, waiting for a time when it could be born and lead us into the dawn of dragon, where we would rule not just the skies but also the land."

"You do realize that sounds like a manifesto for world domination?" For some reason, this made her grin. "Cool."

Her mother arched a brow. "More than cool. It is what should be, given we are, after all, the more evolved species." Long-lived, as well. Not immortal as some human legends would claim, but most of dragonkind lived well into their hundreds, some even made it to two. Although, her great-grandmother Liandra had to be put in a secured chalet—a heavily reinforced one—given she'd gone senile and refused to move from her spot over her hoard of treasure and blasted silver darts at anyone who tried to approach.

"Even if there were an egg, Brand obviously didn't hatch from it." Adi had dug deep enough, as had her Aunts Vanna and Valda, to know that Brandon James Mercer had been born of an actual mother and father. Brand truly did descend from a very long line of gators—and a few snakes—and most certainly wasn't fathered by a dragon. It also wasn't as if he'd suddenly appeared out of nowhere either. His birth, and that of his whole family, was public record. Searches of restricted databases— which were no match for their family's hacking skills—found pictures, school report cards, misdemeanor files, arrest files, even a few warrants for the Mercers, although none were for Brandon.

Interestingly enough, Theodore Parker had filed a missing persons report for Brand. She could almost admire the way his uncle manipulated the humans into working for him to find his nephew.

"The man in my bed might not have been born a dragon, but we shouldn't forget Parker did something to his genes." The information gleaned from rumors stated that Parker made monsters, and most of them went mad.

"You're thinking he spliced dragon genetic matter to Brand's helix," Xylia said with a nod.

"Actually, I was going to say he did a milkshake with his blood and stuff, but your explanation sounds way more science-y."

Her mother shook her head. "A DNA graft or a milkshake, as Aimi—with five years of prep school—calls it, are both unlikely. I cannot see how it would work."

"Science is a scary thing. It can do many things thought impossible. Even merging two species. Look at the hybrid plants the farmers use now. Doing it to a biological entity is not so farfetched, especially since the gator genome sequence and the dragon one are not that dissimilar."

Her mother made a moue of displeasure. "Don't even say it. We are nothing like those filthy mud creatures."

Aimi couldn't help but poke at her mother's disgust. "It's not that bad, Mother. Think of it as the way chimpanzees and humans are alike. We are the more evolved version of both." Just to be a brat, Aimi scratched her armpit.

The first time she did it, her mother froze. The second scratch managed to have her mother utter a loud sigh and turn away.

Score!

"I cannot believe you would think of bringing a swamp creature into the family. What will I tell people?"

"Don't explain. Just stare them down with haughty disdain." Kind of like her mother was doing right now. Aimi grinned. "Just think of the fun we'll have turning him into a snob like us. And you seem to be forgetting something, Mother. Let's say he is a gold. Even if he emerged from perhaps dubious origin, haven't you figured out what that means?"

"He might be the foretold one that those religious fanatics are looking for," her aunt replied with a sage nod of her head.

What? Actually, that wasn't the direction her mind had gone in at all. Damn. One more thing to worry about. But, apparently, her mother still missed the obvious. "I wouldn't be so sure Brand is the one in legend because, in order for Parker to have spliced gold DNA onto Brand, they would have to—"

"—have access to a gold dragon. Or its egg," Xylia said, finishing her thought.

Her mother whirled from the window. "Whichever the case, we need to find it."

And her mother neatly fell into the trap. Aimi slapped her hands on the armrest of the club chair. "I think it's time we paid my fiancé's uncle a visit." Yes, fiancé, because now that her mother was distracted by the possibility of another gold, she would have less time to worry about Aimi's plans, and Aimi's plans included winning a certain challenge with Brand and then claiming him for her hoard. Ahem, she meant claiming him as her husband.

"A visit with Parker?" Her mother mused the idea aloud. "Yes, I think it's past time we paid him a social call. He dares much in his experiments, and even more if he holds our kind hostage. The world needs to know you should never f—"

"—uck."

"—ool around with our kind. Young lady, what is wrong with your mouth today?"

It is dirty, so dirty. It probably deserved that vile spoonful of castor oil that made her stomach rebel in heaving waves, but the gagging was worth it. Aimi had neatly maneuvered her mother into acting against Parker, and it took all she had to hold on to her smirk of triumph as she exited her matriarch's office and did silent fist pumps in the hall. She was still dancing when she got to her sister in the library.

"Judging by your seriously lacking in rhythm

moves, I take it Mother is now giving us the resources to go after Speedy's sister."

"Actually, she thinks we're going after a gold egg. But since that egg is probably wherever Parker is, and Brand's sister is with Parker"—a little jig of happiness— "then, yes, the mission is a go."

"The things you do to manipulate family." Adi shook her head. "Good job, sis. Mom would be so proud if she knew."

"Which she won't because we're not going to tell her." Because Mother Dear probably wouldn't approve of Aimi saving another of those "dirty swamp gators."

Aimi and her sister didn't high-five their win; they swished their hands dragontail-style against each other. Don't judge. They'd been doing it a long time.

"Since the mission is a go, now we just need to choose a location." Adi whirled and began tapping away. "I've actually got three possible places they could be staying. The man owns more than one place. I take it we're keeping our mission a secret and not involving any of the other Septs?"

"Fucking right, we are." Aimi dropped the f-bomb and grinned. "No use letting the other Septs know they might have a treasure in their midst."

"Any idea how we are going to explain to Mother that we're bringing back the sister?"

"I'll figure something out."

"When do you want us to leave?"

We because no way would Adi let Aimi go adventuring on her own. "Right away. Last thing we need is for Mother to change her mind. I take it the cousins are going to tag along, too," Aimi said.

"We are all raring to get out of the house. It's

been a while since we enjoyed a little action."

"Awesome. Let's plan to leave within the hour. I'll just pack a bag and round up Brand." No way was she leaving him behind.

"Speaking of which…hello, what's this?" Adi leaned forward and zoomed one of the security monitors. "Better hurry if you want to hold on to that man of yours because it looks like he's trying to take off without you."

"What do you mean?"

Her sister pointed to a monitor, the one covering the massive garage. Cars of various types filled it, from giant SUVs like the Suburban and the more luxury Escalade to sleek sports cars like the Audi R8 and the newest Mustang model. It also had a wide range of crotch rockets.

The camera zoomed closer, and Aimi clenched her fists as she noted Brand straddling a motorcycle, his profile distinct and quite sexy. Somehow during her absence, he'd managed to clothe himself and had gotten out of a locked room.

The man proved wily, having navigated the mansion's many halls and actually made it undetected to the garage, where he now prepared to flee.

He's running from me.

Hell, no. He's mine.

And this time, she wouldn't lose him to the chase. She barreled out of the library through the garden doors.

It took no thought or effort, just a willing of the change. One moment, she was bound by the tight conscriptions of flesh, and the next, she burst free. The atoms of her expanded, her silvery shape lithe and her tail rapier-tipped. The crested mane flowing from her crown rustled, and strands lifted, dancing in the ghostly wind that always traveled with her.

Her wings unfurled, gossamer thin in appearance, iridescent in sheen, and yet leathery strong. With a fluting note, she sprang to the parapet of the balcony, claws digging into the thick solid stone. The last rays of the sun kissed the horizon, not quite nightfall but close enough.

Here I come, mate. She sprang into the air, a massive goliath unleashed.

In the olden days, when dragons flew, humans hid. In this century, mortals were safe, as the Sept laws prohibited hunting the two-legged. Today, even the cattle could munch without fear as they roamed the massive property. This dragon had another target in sight.

Brand. Oh, Brand.

She hummed his name and saw his head jerk, but he stayed his course, the bike speeding down the long driveway. How droll. He thought he could escape.

Not today.

One massive sweep of her wings, and she coasted over him, casting a shadow that caused him to crane his head. She saw his lips move—*What the fuck?*—and felt his astonishment through the link binding them.

The bike wobbled as he lost control. Addled by her magnificence more than likely. Her family did have the most striking scales of all the Septs.

A graceful dive brought her within reach just as he righted the weaving bike. His perch on the seat made it easy for her to snatch him with her claws, much like a bird of prey and its dinner. A few strokes

Eve Langlais

of her wings, and she was moving higher into the sky. When she reached the right altitude, she banked and headed back toward the house then past it. She wanted a talk with her mate, in private, and she knew just the place.

The wind rushing past stole all the protests he made, and she ignored the irritation radiating from his mind. However, she couldn't ignore the earful Brand yelled at her when she dropped him in the pool of natural spring water.

She chose to land upon a large boulder before shifting shape.

He kicked to the surface, sputtering and yelling. "You're a fucking dragon."

About time he noticed.

Chapter Nine

A dragon. Aimi was a fucking dragon. And her reply to this most momentous of news?

"Duh. I told you so."

He swam to the edge of the pool and sloshed out. "No, you can't be. You were supposed to be some crazy girl with delusions of being a fucking dragon. Not a real fucking dragon." Such a beautiful one, too. When he'd seen the shadow overhead, noticeable even with the falling twilight, he'd suspected it was Aimi, but he could have never imagined the rest.

Cartoons often portrayed dragons as sporting fat bellies and spewing flames, wearing horns with smoke curling from their nostrils. Some also sang— Puff the magic dragon anyone? The truth about dragons proved somewhere in the middle.

Aimi's beast held a lithe shape, more serpentine slender than rounded belly. While she still had two legs and two arms, they were hinged slightly different, and her toes sported sharp claws—*that dangled me like a worm on a hook*. His mancard sobbed in his pocket.

Her scales were incredible, appearing made of actual silver, bright and flashy. He wondered how she'd look with her skin refracting the setting rays of the sun.

I look beautiful. "Before you ask, you spoke aloud, not in your head."

Despite her claim, he still gave her a stiff-lipped stare. She didn't look like a dragon now. Even her eyes were normal and human looking. He suspected her pupils only slitted green fire when her beast pushed.

"You're a fucking dragon." He couldn't help but repeat himself.

"I don't know why you're acting so surprised. I told you from the start what I was. You were the one who kept insisting I lied." She shrugged, the movement sending a ripple through the hair forming a silvery curtain around her body. Her nude body. Parts of it flashed as her hair shimmered over her skin. Hide and seek. A game he wanted to play with his lips and hands through the silk skeins of her tresses.

Want her. He most certainly did. Wanted her for himself. The pretty-shiny precious moonbeam who'd suddenly appeared in his life.

A woman who was a dragon.

"Dragons aren't fucking real." A denial that no longer worked. He'd seen Aimi in all her gleaming beauty. Such a majestic creature. Few things awed him. She did, though; a strange new feeling for him.

And he'd thought to touch her? Kiss her? He wasn't worthy of her. Not by a long shot.

"Let us recap so you can stop repeating yourself. I am a dragon. Dragons are real. Want to touch me again to be sure?" A teasing smile lifted the corners of her lips, and her hip jutted to the left, loosing the silken hair covering it. Even with the murky shadows, he could see her exposed skin.

How he wanted to touch her and do dirty, wicked things to her body. *Have her scream my name as she comes for me.* A wickedly appealing fantasy, but one he couldn't have. "Fuck me."

"I'm ready now if you are." She took a step forward.

The temptation almost dropped him to his knees. *On my knees, I could worship her as she deserves.* A true moon goddess who entranced him. "I can't."

"You mean you won't because we both know you can." Her gaze dropped to a spot below his belt.

"Don't you look at me like that. I was more than willing earlier, and then you drugged me."

"My sister drugged you. For your own safety."

"How is making me helpless safe?"

"Because then you don't do stupid things like try and leave." She glared and pouted at the same time. A powerful combo.

Not going to kiss her. Nope, not him. He was still pissed. With good reason. He'd woken from a drugged sleep to find himself locked in a room. The result proved to be a litany of curses—goddamn piss fucking son of a bastard—that did nothing to get him out.

However, he'd learned a thing or two about electronic door locks while working at Bittech. There was always a way to shut it down and open the door manually—unlike the movies.

"I left because you had no right to keep me prisoner."

"You're my mate."

"Well, you sure didn't act like it."

"Did you not wake in my bed with me?"

"Do you lock in all your lovers?"

She smiled. "Only the one I'm keeping. Congrats, you're the first."

The words shouldn't have warmed him. Why didn't he fight their allure? *Shut the fuck up and enjoy it.*

Nothing wrong with enjoying the fact that a woman appreciated him. He'd had to wash that appreciation off his hand so it wouldn't give him away when he made his escape.

A male should never share the scent of his woman's passion. It's mine and mine alone. Sharing was for saps.

"You know, if a guy does the same thing, it's considered a felony."

"Sucks to have a penis."

He winced. "You shouldn't use that word."

"What word? Penis?" Cringe. She laughed. "I don't believe it. He cowers at the word penis."

"I don't cower," he said, lips twisted in annoyance.

"Penis."

Flinch. Glare.

"Peeeee-nnnnnissss." She sang it.

"I don't care if you're a dragon. Say it one more time, and I'll put you over my knee and spank you."

"Promise?" She batted her lashes, which were dark, unlike her hair. "What word should I use instead? Penis is the proper word."

"Cock." The word burst from him, reasserting some manhood to his manbits. "Dick. Giant lizard."

"Lizard? You think lizard is a sexier option to penis?" She stared at him, mouth agape.

"Snake also works, as does love shaft, boner, and dong. They're okay, too, depending on how you use them."

"There is another term mother approves of—baby maker."

Funny how that didn't make him flinch. "There will be no baby making."

"Don't let my mother hear you say that."

He blinked at her. "Your mother wants me to fuck you?"

"That's the preferred method of getting pregnant. By the way, I feel like I should mention, she hates the f-word."

"Your mother can kiss my ass."

"She just might if it turns out you're really a gold."

Ah, yes, the insane belief that he was a dragon. As if. He could never aspire to the beauty he'd seen. A gator or a freak with wings was his lot in life. At this point, he wasn't even sure he still had the ability to change. The only thing certain was that the cold voice within still spoke to him and, even more worrisome, appeared to be blending in.

"What if you're wrong? What if I'm not gold? What then?" He already knew the answer. They'd cast him out faster than a drunk at a bar at closing time.

"If you're not, then, as a consolation prize, you can kiss my butt instead." She smiled. "Or bite it. I'm open either way."

Why did she make it so hard? And he meant hard. Any chance she didn't know the effect she had on him? Judging by her coy smile...no, she knew. "You're trying to distract me again."

"Is it working?"

It worked all too well. As Aimi stepped off

the massive rock, her hair wisped around her body, teasing and revealing only snippets of her perfection.

"You're naked." The observation from before spilled past his lips.

"Your grasp of the obvious is startling."

"I didn't mean it that way. I mean you have no clothes, even though you changed back. From watching movies and stuff, I thought dragons weren't like shifters. I thought you were supposed to be more magic. Shouldn't that mean you keep your clothes when you morph?"

"It would certainly make things easier if we could. Alas, we are perhaps more like Cryptos than we like to believe."

"Cryptos?"

"Short for Cryptozoids. It is what we call those who are not dragon or human."

The line dividing him from her got thicker. He was but a shifter whose entire belief system had gotten turned upside down. "Your culture is completely different from mine, isn't it?"

"Yes. We have a unique way of living, much of it very structured, but many of our laws came about out of a need for survival after the purge."

"The purge being…?"

"When humans tried to hunt us to extinction. Much like what might happen now that the Cryptozoids have revealed themselves to humanity."

"You think they'll kill us all?"

"I should hope not because it would mean we would never have a hope of revealing ourselves."

"And do dragons *want* to reveal themselves?" he asked.

"I think most of us just want to be able to fly

free in the sun and blue skies once again."

"You did just now." A setting sun, but still, it was far from dark outside.

"And for that, I will probably be punished. Even though I did it in a safe spot, I broke a cardinal rule."

"The rebel of the family, are you?"

She appeared startled by his statements. "Me? No. That's usually my sister, Adi."

"And yet, your sister isn't the one here on this mountain with me."

"Of course, she isn't. I claimed you."

The nonchalance with which she threw that at him didn't detract from the words themselves. "Should I be flattered?"

"Are you looking for compliments?" Her lips curved. "I claimed you because you intrigue me. It is hard enough to find an unmated male, but to find one who is handsome and strong and not a mama's boy…" She reached out a hand to trace his lower lip. "That was not a prize I could ignore."

"I won't be owned." His uncle and Andrew and Bittech had thought to own him once upon a time. He wouldn't let that happen again.

"But I take ever such good care of my things. Wait until you see my hoard."

"Hold on a second, did you just say—"

"You talk too much. Come here." She grabbed his chin and pulled him down, and he let her, mostly because staring into those shockingly beautiful violet eyes, he couldn't stop himself.

"You're dangerous, moonbeam." His words dusted her lips; her hands cradled his cheeks.

The reply hit him warmly. "Thank you.

Remember that if you ever decide to cross me. Apparently, my family still has yet to learn how to give me my space."

Whirling from him, she planted her hands on her hips and yelled at the approaching drone. "Yes, I know I'm in trouble. But could you give me fifteen minutes with my mate?"

Fifteen? He could probably shave that down to five for both of them.

Zap. The streak of heat hit the ground at her bare feet, and Aimi scowled. "You pussy-blocking, womb-hogging, ass-kissing traitor. I will get you back for this."

Zap. Aimi easily dodged the laser's streak. "We'll have to continue this conversation later."

"Or I could grab that drone and make it into scrap." It occurred to him that chivalry demanded he destroy the toy robot.

"She'll just send another. Besides, we should get back. We have a mission."

"A mission? To do what?" Finish what they started?

"You still want to save your sister?"

"Yes." The mention of Sue-Ellen had him forgetting any thoughts of seduction. Sue-Ellen was the reason he'd left the house in the first place. "Do you have a clue as to her whereabouts?"

"Not quite but I'm sure it won't be long before we've pinpointed it for sure."

"What my so-in-trouble twin means to say," said a tinny voice issuing from the drone, "is that she has an invitation to the gala one Sue-Ellen Mercer is attending tonight in Beverly Hills. And guess who gets to be Aimi's plus one?"

"I'm going to see my sister?" The very concept stunned.

"Apparently. So let's go."

And by *go*, Aimi meant now, as with a shimmer, she went from seductress to dragoness— silver-scaled majesty.

Stunningly beautiful.

Don't touch.

Fuck it, he touched, the scales warm against his skin and of the strangest texture.

"Mom is going to kill you," sang Aimi's twin, to which Aimi replied by swatting the drone out of the sky.

He, on the other hand, was emasculated as once again she grabbed him in her claws and carried him, with ease he might add.

How did such a tiny woman pack such a large creature? It made no sense.

He got a chance to ask less than two hours later when they were on board a plane to the West Coast. First class, of course, a section overtaken by mostly platinum hair. Apparently, as a Silvergrace, Aimi required an entourage, whereas Brandon needed a lead suit, given he was pretty sure a few of the cousins who'd bummed along had x-ray stares.

To ignore them, he chose to talk to the seductress seated by his side. "How is your dragon so large?"

"That's a rude question." Bright eyes peered at him over the headrest in front. "I'm sure you wouldn't hear Aimi asking how your dick got so big."

Aimi dove forward and grabbed—was it cousin Deka or Babette?—by the hair and growled. "Don't you be looking at my mate's parts. *Mine.*"

"You can keep him. I hear he's quick in the sack."

His turn to feel heat warming his cheeks. He bit back his retort of, "You'd come quick, too, if you hadn't truly touched a woman in two years." But it was more than just that. Aimi just excited him that much. She also fascinated him, especially how she went from being such a proper lady to wild-eyed hoyden banging her cousin's head off the seat.

"Aimi! Let her go," shouted someone a row behind. "You know the airlines frown on blood."

With one last growl and tug, Aimi released her cousin, who slunk back into her seat. It didn't stop his moonbeam from muttering, "Next time you look at him, I'm eating your eyeballs."

Some people might have taken her literally, but Brandon, used to these kinds of family interactions, thought nothing of it. Mercer celebrations usually involved a few brawls, blood, and loose teeth. To prevent any more trouble, he diverted her attention, drawing it to him instead. "Okay, Captain Cavedragon, did you seriously just say 'mine?' Isn't that right up there with 'I licked it?'" He might act aggrieved, but there was definitely something hot about a woman—not just any woman, but Aimi—saying that.

"Yup." She shrugged. "Dragons tend to have a hoarding gene. Once you ascend, you'll feel it, too."

Why wait? I already covet a certain moonbeam for my own.

He waited for his colder self to add in its two cents and was surprised when it remained silent. It hadn't said much since his change to his man shape. Did his gator sulk?

I'm here. Even more than before. Cryptic words that he didn't have time for. The rescue for Sue-Ellen took precedence over everything. "So what is this party we're going to that has my sister attending?"

"You don't have any idea at all what date it is, do you?"

"No. Why?" He frowned. He'd lost track of a lot of things during his run-and-hide routine the past few months.

"Does November third ring a bell?"

November third. "Ah, fuck. It's Sue-Ellen's birthday. You mean this is a party for her?"

"Yes."

"But how did you get invited? I thought you didn't know her or Parker."

"I don't, but Mother does, and since the birthday party is also acting as a fundraiser to request funds to promote a better relationship between shifters and humans, we got an invite."

"Back up a second. I thought people didn't know you were dragons."

"They don't, but we have loads of money."

"An invitation is all well and good, but you can't seriously expect us to just walk in. I have a feeling Parker is still gunning for me." Of course, his uncle wanted back the pet project that had gotten away. *Uncle Theo wants his slave.* He fisted his hands by his side rather than let them touch his bare neck. He'd had such a hard time getting the controlling collar off, he had no interest in wearing one again.

"Of course, we won't just walk in." She gave him a duh tone and expression. "We're dragon. We strut."

The assertion made him grin. "You've got

balls, moonbeam, I'll give you that, but I don't know if this is a good idea, confronting him like that. Uncle Theo will probably have security in place with orders to watch out for me." A covert operation to extract his sister seemed like a wiser move.

"Don't you worry about your uncle. Why do you think we got so many volunteers to come? They're expecting trouble. We're going to have so much fun."

"You're going to fight? I thought you dragon gals liked to stay low-key. You do know there will be cameras there."

A coy smile tilted her lips. "There are cameras everywhere we go, and yet, you won't see many images of us around."

"You won't be able to avoid being caught out tonight if you start shit. It's not just cameras you have to worry about. Keep in mind, Parker won't hesitate to shove you out of the closet."

"Parker might be many things, but he's not stupid. If he outs us, it will be the last thing he ever does, and he knows that. But at the same time, he can't be allowed to continue with his impunity, especially if it turns out he's been using us to experiment. We shall crush him." She slammed a fist into her palm and wore the most savage smile.

It was so fucking hot. "Crush him like a bug? Can I watch? I'd love to see him demolished by a girl."

"I'd love to knock him toothless, too. Alas, that would draw too much attention."

"Then how are you going to crush him?"

"Not all fights are physical. We're going to demolish Parker with elegance."

"Sounds civilized," he said with a moue of displeasure.

"Have you ever seen someone socially ruined?" She arched a brow.

"All the time in high school."

She made a noise. "That is mere bullying. This is an art. You'll see."

What he saw was a bunch of excited women, treating this excursion as a lark. It struck him in that moment what a grave disservice he might be doing to the Silvergrace ladies, drawing them into danger. What if Parker decided to take Aimi or one of her other family members hostage to use in more of his experiments? Aimi could pretend all she wanted that Parker wouldn't dare, but Brandon didn't doubt for a second Parker would do whatever he wanted if he thought it would serve him.

"I should be going on this mission alone."

"Are you ashamed of me?"

"What? No?" More like he didn't want the responsibility of keeping them out of his uncle's clutches.

"If you're not ashamed, then why wouldn't you want me to go with you?"

"None of you should be going with me. Don't you realize what kind of danger we're talking about? My uncle, Theo, is the guy who had no problem blackmailing family. Who experimented on me and countless others. Dragon or not, Theo won't hesitate to harm you. What if I can't protect you?" Just like he hadn't protected his sister. What if he failed again?

Failure is not an option. Next time, we crunch.

"Aw, isn't that sweet. He thinks we might get hurt. Don't you worry about us, Speedy," Adi chided as she walked past. "We can take care of ourselves, and we'll keep your butt safe, too."

He frowned. "Why is she calling me Speedy?"

"You really don't want to know."

Except the way she said it caused him to understand and his cheeks flamed. Doing something about it, though, meant hitting a girl, Aimi's twin. *Fuck me.*

Since the flight they were booked on was an overnight one, he closed his eyes and relished the feel of Aimi using him as a body pillow. He let his mind wander, wondering if his luck were about to change. Could his bad streak finally be coming to an end?

After more than two long years, would he reunite with his little sister? *I'm not a monster anymore. I can have a life. A normal life.*

Normal isss overrated, and things would be better if monsters ruled the world. Monstersss like me.

I'm not a monster.

The coldness swirled around him, drawing him into a place of smoke and shadows, a place in his mind where he and his beast cohabited.

You are more than a man, and yet you keep trying to deny what you are.

And what am I? He wasn't sure anymore.

You and the thing you would call monster are one, and you need to stop fighting it.

I am me!

You are the dragon we seek. We see you. We come.

The strange voice spoke within his dream, jarring him as it forced its alien presence into his reality.

His eyes shot wide open, the sleep he'd fallen into wiped in an instant. He immediately wondered if he'd imagined it. The subconscious was a powerful place, or so his great-nana told him. She believed in portents and messages via the dreamworld. She also believed in a few glasses of moonshine before bed.

The voice didn't speak again, and around him, he noted no panic or agitation. Leaning against his arm, Aimi still snoozed. It seemed everyone did judging by the soft snores. What didn't sleep was his bladder.

Easing out from under Aimi, he stood and stretched. First class gave him enough room to squeeze past her without having to wake her up. She cutely grumbled anyhow at the loss of her pillow.

The bathroom at the front of the plane said *Occupied*. Since he didn't mind stretching his legs, he went through the curtain and headed to the one at the back, noting the passengers in this area as he did. It was less than a third full, and only a few were awake, reading by feeble lights. No one paid him any mind.

Not normal.

Paranoia, his dear friend, wanted to make an issue of it. He, on the other hand, was more interested in the pair of bathrooms at the far end. One was available.

It took some maneuvering to get into the slim cubicle, as it was made for tiny people. He finally managed to wedge the door shut, slide the lock to *Occupied*, and whip it out.

Midstream, the plane rocked, and he missed, pulling a rookie splash. "Fuck." He finished, did a quick wipe, and washed his hands before exiting. The plane wobbled again. Damned turbulence.

As he made his way up the aisle, he noted

more than a few lights on, and some of the passengers peering out the windows. Of more interest, their whispers,

"What is that?"

"Is it a giant bird?"

"Looks like gargoyles to me."

That last remark brought a chill to his blood. He leaned down and did his best to peek. The sky outside remained dark, so dark, with only the lights on the plane's wings to illuminate it, which was enough to see a bulky shape on the metal, a shape that moved.

"Monster!" The word that started the panic.

Beep. Beep. Beep. Alarms went off as people paged the flight attendant. As for Brandon, he suddenly realized what the shape on the wing was.

The plane was being attacked by…

"Dragons!"

Chapter Ten

The bellowed word hit Aimi's consciousness, and she went instantly awake. She wasn't the only one his yell had triggered. In a blink, she noted a few things, the most important being Brandon gone from his seat, but a gentle tug on her bond showed him not far away.

However, the chaotic mix of his thoughts didn't reassure. He saw something outside of the plane. A dragon, here at thirty thousand feet? Impossible.

Yet, why did the plane wobble?

Turbulence perhaps. The pilot screwing with them. Or, as a quick peek showed, a hunched and winged figure pulling a gremlin on the wings, hopping up and down, causing some screams.

Before she could even process the improbability of an attack at this altitude, someone yanked on the emergency door mid ship, releasing the seal, and that was when all hell broke loose. Actually, everything that was loose went sucking toward the breach in the cabin.

Many of the humans in economy lost their shit, but Aimi and the other Silvergrace girls were made of tougher stuff. Pushing and shoving—but politely, "Please get out of my way, heifer."—the girls bolted toward the commotion, letting the suction draw them, their hair whipping around their heads in a halo.

The wild style did not block her view, though, so Aimi clearly saw the smirking redhead, a male about mid-thirties, balding and freckled, grappling with Brand. Behind them, a gaping hole where the emergency door used to be.

"Why did you open it?" she heard her mate yell.

"Glory be to the Crimson Sept, keepers of the Golden Faith." The ginger-haired fellow pushed away from Brand and flung himself through the sucking hole.

"What the fuck?" Brand braced himself in the aisle, gripping the seats, using his strength to hold himself in place against the wild suction.

Claws gripped the edges of the exit door, followed by a poking serpentine head, ridged and bright red, the eyes a malevolent yellow.

A wyvern. How unexpected.

"Girls, we have company," she sang as she released the seats she gripped and let herself arrow feet first toward the creature trying to board. She got there too late. A human, who hadn't buckled like the flashing signs all warned, hit the intruder first. They both flew out the opening, and Aimi followed.

She heard Brand shout, "What the fuck are you doing, moonbeam? Get back in here." The panic oozing from him made her smile.

Would you look at that, he cares. Behind her, she could hear the shrill cries of her sister and cousins. It seemed the wyvern on board hadn't come alone. She saw a red shape streak past the doorway

A wyvern shifting in plain sight? She could only imagine what kind of media mess that would cause. But they'd worry about that later. Someone had been brazen enough to strike while they were in the air. A dragon Sept had broken the rules of their kind. The Crimson Sept had attacked, and that demanded a reply. A very pointed and deadly answer.

Aimi gave little thought to clothes when she shimmered into her silvery shape. Who had the time to care about puny fabric trappings when the most beautiful scales adorned her body?

She swooped through the air in time to catch her adversary, a flame-colored wyvern, landing atop the plane. Smaller than true dragons, with heavier haunches, smaller heads, and no innate power, wyverns were the result of a dragon and human pairing. It was heavily frowned upon, as wyverns were half-breeds, incapable of breeding, and not good for much but foot soldier positions. One advantage they did have? Their lack of scent in human shape made them hard to spot as spies. Their major disadvantage? They were quite feral and violent, the biggest reason why their creation was more or less banned.

It seemed the reds were playing with more than just fire these days. The wyvern let out a shrill cry, a coarse sound that lacked the dulcet tone of a true-born.

She replied with a trumpeting flute, the notes piercingly bright. They were also a challenge. With a scream, the wyvern came at her, only to find itself knocked off course as Babette tackled it. Her silver frame was streaked with blue, a hint of her father in her scales.

As her cousin took care of the interloper, Aimi peeked around for its cohorts. She already knew one wyvern wouldn't attack alone, especially against a half-dozen Silvergraces. She knew there were a few on board, tangling with her family, but she suspected there were others outside the plane, too. Why else open the door?

She dipped under the aircraft, and her eyes widened as she noted the bodies in the sky flapping toward them, the many bodies, and that wasn't counting the ones that suddenly perched on the plane's wing. The weight of it unbalanced things, and the nose of the plane dipped. Sweeping past the belly of the craft, she tipped up the other side to see another pair of wyverns on the wings, going after the second hatch and managing to tear it loose.

Nothing came flying out, the first breach having suctioned all the loose items, including at least one unlucky passenger.

There was only one thing left on board without a buckle. Brand!

Before Aimi could head to the plane, some of the arriving wyvern fleet saw her and banked in her direction, uttering shrill war cries.

You want to fight? Bring it. Uttering her own clarion, she swept in to attack.

Aerial fights sounded great in theory. Looked even more awesome on screen. But in reality, they were chaos.

Winds fought against fighting pairs, tugging at their wings, trying to tumble them. They grappled with claws, swiping and trying to grab, and yet, at the same time, being careful not to lock, lest their wings tangle and they both plummet to their deaths.

Gravity also played a huge part as it tugged at their weight. They might have the pounds they condensed as a human expanded as a dragon, their bones lightweight and hollow yet tungsten strong, but any kind of weight was subject to gravity.

As Aunt Waida often claimed, "What goes up, always comes down and splats."

Watching the earth approach at breakneck speed was never fun, not with the memory of her aunt slapping her fist into her hand and making a squishy sound. A good thing an uncontrolled dive was the first lesson a mother taught her dragonling. The first time it had happened, Aimi could at least say she hadn't peed herself, but her lunch hadn't fared so well, and neither had the cow it landed on. Cousin Jackie from the Silverheart Sept never did forgive her on account she was munching on said cow at the time.

But Aimi was a big girl now, and while she didn't have the experience her ancestors did when it came to an airborne fight, she could hold her lunch and her own against a smaller wyvern. Unless there were several attacking at once.

Little bastards. Since they tried to swarm, she screwed with them, letting herself drop straight down and then flipping to her back. She caught the first wyvern by surprise and gutted it, her claws more than just pretty. Adi slammed into a second, easily recognizable even without their bond, given Adi's dragon form had a short pink ruff on her neck. As for the third wyvern who thought to play unfair? Aimi had to chase it.

As she got within arm's reach, a shrill bugle of a cry had her putting on the brakes midair.

What's this? A late arrival?

She craned her head, her long neck twisting, and noted an attacker, a red dragon hovering just outside the plane and the breach.

Aha, there's the culprit behind the attack. And, apparently, the attack had nothing to do with the Silver Sept and everything to do with her mate. A pair of wyverns shoved Brand into the door. He faced them with his back straight, and was it her, or did he give them the finger and utter, "Fuck you. Come and get me."

Undaunted. Fearless. *And mine.*

Until the dragon reached out and snatched her man from the plane. That would not do at all.

He belongs to me. Time to get him back.

Except, Brand freed himself before she could reach him, his closed fist pounding at the claws holding him until, with a screech, the dragon let go, and Brand fell.

I'd better catch him. A plan that would have worked better if the red dragon hadn't spotted her and uttered a challenge.

I don't have time for this. The dragoness didn't care. She slammed into Aimi and hissed. Nice of her to bring the fight, but Aimi wasn't in the mood, not with Brand free falling and not in a good Tom Petty kind of way.

Let me go. She struggled with the other dragon, the red viper belching obnoxious fumes in her face, and Aimi could only hope she'd already spat her fire, and the flames were now extinguished. Unlike the storybooks, dragons didn't have an unlimited supply. A good thing, or she might have needed a vat of aloe to soothe her burned face.

Their wings flapped and tucked, alternatively keeping them aloft and coasting the high winds at this altitude, but gravity also pulled, forcing them to flutter lest they get drawn into a death spiral.

Their breaths grew short. They couldn't wrestle forever, especially since the longer it took, the farther her mate fell.

Scraping Brand off pavement didn't seem like a good way to start married life.

Enough. Aimi didn't use her dragon power often. None of the pure-blooded Silvergrace did because it was so deadly and final. Their particular family Sept wasn't one of the most powerful families for nothing. Their breath could impart death.

Bye bye, bitch.

Aimi pulled from inside herself, pulled at that core within that made her dragon, the silver essence of herself. It tingled.

She blew, exhaled deeply, and let the flaps within her throat open, drawing through them the venom she carried. All dragons had some kind of *special power.* A poisonous gas, acid, flame, and even ice.

One branch of silver had the Midas Curse, and yes, it was related to the fable humans told, except the Midas legend had gotten a few things wrong in the retelling. First, Midas was a dragon—an uncle several times removed. He was also a king, a conquering one, who turned all those who thought to thwart him to silver—not gold. It turned out to be a lot of people until, one day, he found himself all alone, with only silver statues of people, expressions still screaming, left to keep him company.

Then there were those with the Silver Rain

gift. They could literally spit machine gun fire. The Silverleafs? They could shape silver, using it to cage their enemy or create a fine lattice for sale.

As for the Silvergraces, their power was the nastiest of all. They had the Dust.

As Aimi breathed out, she saw the horror in the other dragon's eyes. The backpedaling as, suddenly, it recognized its mortality.

Too late.

Her exhalation puffed fine particles onto the other dragon. It seemed so innocuous at first. A dust that the opponent sucked in. It didn't hurt, not one bit, and yet, they were dead as soon as they inhaled.

Much like a virus, the Dust spread to living tissue, consuming and killing it. Worse than killing it, it crumbled into…nothingness.

The red squealed as the Dust took hold, and the reaction was instantaneous. Pieces of the other dragon flaked away, fluttering much like ash. The red dragon thrashed in the air, her color turning gray as more and more of her succumbed to the wasting death.

Back in the day, according to her Aunt Waida, the humans had called it the unmaking, which Adi declared was so much cooler sounding than the Dust, but no matter the name, none affected ever survived.

With her foe no longer a problem, Aimi focused on Brand, a mere speck too far below her. She plummeted toward him, feeling the yank of gravity hastening her plunge. The wind streamed hard into her face, pushing against her second eyelids, the thin membrane that covered her orbs from damage during flight. Her wings were tucked tight to her body, making her as small as possible, anything to streamline her descent.

She moved fast toward the earth, but it wasn't enough; she wouldn't reach him in time. Failure was unacceptable, and she uttered a fluted cry of frustration.

And got a reply.

Don't worry, moonbeam. I got this.

Chapter Eleven

The reassurance he broadcast at Aimi—because somehow, he felt her worry for him—was perhaps a tad more confident than Brandon actually felt. Then again, he needed confidence right now.

Plummeting to the ground gave a man time to reflect on things, such as vowing to never pass up a chance to eat cheeseburgers slathered in every condiment known to man from a fast food truck. He also needed to visit the Grand Canyon and see a sunset just because he'd always thought it looked cool on television. But the thing he still wanted to do most? Fuck moonbeam within an inch of her life because he felt like a moron for passing up the chance.

All the optimism and confidence in the world couldn't hide the fact that he was going to die—smashed into the ground, creating a Brandon slurry. He saw his demise in her frantic flight, heard it in the panic oozing somehow from her to him.

And then it occurred to him.

I can fly, too. At least he used to, but the question was, could he change shapes, back into the hybrid one he'd met Aimi in?

Is anybody in there?

For a second, he could hear shades of Pink

Floyd in that phrase.

Yes. I am always here.

He noticed how his gator's words didn't seem to roll the S's anymore. When had it learned to control its accent?

There is no it *anymore. Me, myself, and I are one.*

Not quite the sanest thing he'd ever heard, but no point quibbling. *Want to give me a hand here?*

Don't you mean a wing?

Whatever. Didn't it figure his other side had lost its accent and acquired a sense of humor.

He closed his eyes, mostly to ignore the earth rushing at him. Arms and legs spread wide could only do so much to slow a man's descent.

At first, he felt nothing. *Why isn't this working?* He forced himself to shut down the outside world and tug on that part of him inside that used to house his beast, except it wasn't there.

Where had it gone?

Everything is one now.

There it was again, that assertion that they weren't two entities. What a strange concept. He and his beast had always each had thoughts, distinct ones, while sharing one body.

Not sharing. Not anymore.

It implied there was no line between man and beast.

Not implying, stating.

All is one.

If true, then flipping shapes should be as simple as moving a limb.

Snap. Ouch. Still fucking painful, too.

The bad news, he lost his damned shirt, and it was chilly enough to make nipples cut glass. The good news?

I've got wings. Whoosh. He banked on the air currents, a gradual loop so as to take his momentum into account. His wings extended, catching air.

You didn't die!

The exuberant exclamation hit him almost physically, and he recoiled. He peered upward and, despite the dark night sky, saw a silver streak heading for him.

No way was he letting her grab him again. He'd been emasculated enough for one day.

Where are you going? she asked. *We have to return to the plane.*

Back onto that death trap? No, thank you.

No, thank you? How polite.

Did she just read his thoughts?

Not exactly. It's more like you don't hide them very well.

Did that mean everyone could hear him? How utterly appalling.

Not everyone. Only me, on account we are connected.

"Are you telling me I hear you because I'm reading your thoughts?" Brand spoke out loud because the mind thing just seemed freakishly wrong.

You hear only the thoughts I'm projecting at you.

Like this? He squinted his eyes and projected one message. *Don't grab me like a mouse.*

No need to shout. I hear you fine, and you hear me fine, and I won't grab you if you stop flying away and come back with me to the plane.

The problem with following her back was that the plane didn't seem too safe right now. He could see it angling toward the ground, looking to make an emergency stop. Only an idiot would go back on board, or—he glanced at her and noted her craning toward the plane—someone who had family still within.

"Let's go save them."

Save them? Her mental query sounded genuinely confused. *Save them from what?*

"Crashing. Death." When she blinked at him, with a translucent set of eyelids, he added more clues. "As in fiery ball of doom. *Kaboom.*" He blew up his hands.

She laughed, a trilling sound as she dove and wove around him, her body undulating on the air currents, close and yet not touching him.

It was oddly erotic.

The plane is not blowing up. There is plenty of open space for landing in this area. And even if it did look like it might hit hard, we're not wilting flowers. We are Silvergrace. We would survive. We always survive.

How ominous sounding. But in a sense, it reminded him of the Mercer clan. As his grand-mère often said, "Yeah, we get shit on, but when it happens, we always rise above and manage to whoop some tail."

"Well, if you're not worried about them at all, then why do you want to rejoin them? I, for one, would prefer to ditch the plane. Falling from way too many thousands of feet isn't something I'm in the mood to repeat."

I'm sure there are no wyverns left to cause trouble.

"Wyverns being?"

The smaller, much less awesome creatures.

"And the one you fought at the end, it was a dragon, like you?" He might have been falling, but he couldn't help but catch parts of what had happened between Aimi and the red adversary.

The other dragon was gone. Just ashed into flakes and blown away.

That was a red dragon, not as lovely as me, of course. Nor as talented, given I won the battle. Was it him, or did the silver dragon do a fist pump? Or was that claw?

It should have terrified him the kind of power she had. It should have, at the very least, inspired a scratch of his balls—which was totally less satisfying in this hybrid shape, given they were tucked inside with a good portion of his cock. Traumatizing when he'd first seen it, and he'd gone into a minor depression over them shrinking his dick.

I am pleased to announce I am still just as big as ever. Make that bigger.

"I say we ditch your family and go do this thing on our own."

Okay. Her reply came immediately.

That seemed rather easy. Then again, perhaps she said yes for a reason. Ditching the Silvergrace girls on board now would save them from getting involved. Great plan. However, it still left Aimi in danger. *I need to keep her safe.*

Or he could trust that she was even tougher than him and not likely to be happy if he did anything to cut her out of the action. Chivalry warred with her happiness.

Protecting her would piss her off. It said he thought her incapable of being his partner. Thing was, he knew she could handle it. Probably better than he could. Look at how well she'd handled the attack. No tears or hysterics, no wild flailing with a frying pan or using silver buckshot. Aimi fought, no weapon but herself. And she'd won.

Only an idiot wouldn't want her playing on his team.

Still, he had to try. "Are you sure you want to ditch them? I thought you wanted your sister and cousins to tag along on this birthday party mission."

More glory and reward for us if we handle it ourselves.

Good point. Funny how his agreeing didn't seem strange at all. Then again, who wouldn't want more rewards?

Speaking of getting something valuable, he flipped to his back, letting his wings flutter and fan the air so he could see Aimi coasting alongside him on the current. He couldn't deny how nice he found it.

It wasn't the first time he'd flown with someone, but he preferred to forget about the rabid freak Bittech tried to pair him with. A few missions with that psycho reptile—a failed version of Brandon, as his uncle liked to remind him—had been enough to make him see the merit in putting down rabid pets.

Flying with Aimi proved interesting, first because he felt kind of small beside her. Yet, at the same time, he didn't get an impression of overwhelming weight as she skimmed over him, her frame casting a shadow as it blocked starlight.

"I don't think I ever did get an explanation of how you can be so big. I've seen some people defy the laws of science, especially the bear breeds, those are some big dudes, but their bears are even bigger. But you, you're the size of a—"

Say house, and I will eat you.

"—house. Let me know what time you're dining and I'll drop my pants." It was probably the most brazen thing he'd said to a woman in years, perhaps ever. Rude. Crude. And for some reason, he thought it ridiculously funny. So he laughed.

To his surprise, she sent him mental chuckles, and in that moment, he realized an interesting thing. Aimi might be a dragon, but she was still the woman he'd met, too. What she could become did not take away from her droll sense of humor and single-mindedness. He found himself rather in awe of her, and in lust. He also totally coveted her. *A silver prize to start my hoard. I shall find her jewels to enhance her beauty. Fine silks to caress her body.*

What the hell? He shook his head.

Is there a problem, Brand? she asked.

Yeah, there was because he now couldn't help but think of her in terms of possession, as in keeping. When did that start to happen?

Probably because she kept insisting he belonged to her. He just couldn't figure out why she wanted him.

What does she see in me?

He'd forgotten about their link and so could have punched something in embarrassment when she replied, *I see a sexy hunk of treasure.*

Chapter Twelve

Sexy hunk of treasure? Who the hell said that? *What am I, in seventh grade?* No wonder he flipped around and ignored her.

Problem was, he totally pushed all her buttons. He was sexy. Very hunky, and a treasure she wanted to worship with her mouth and tongue.

The things I want to do to you. And he pretended as if she weren't there.

No. Not happening. *Have you forgotten the lesson about the world?*

"Yeah, about that." Brand flipped onto his back again, showcasing the rippling muscles of his chest, the way his pants hung low on his hips. She might have gotten a little hung up on the vee.

He had a nice vee. Drool.

Want it.

Oops, she might have projected that thought, because his eyes widened. Then he grinned.

"Then come and get it."

A challenge? She might have slobbered some more. He truly knew how to tease her.

She swooped low and reached out to grab him, only to have him dart out of her grasp.

He also taunted. "Too slow."

I am just warming up. I don't want to end things too

quickly.

"But fast and furious can be fun. I still remember the feel of you on my fingers."

The distracting reminder of the pleasure caused her to wobble. He did it on purpose to stay out of reach. No more. She would show him.

Banking left, she went to snare him again, only to have him bob at the last second and pop up behind her, giving her tail a yank.

You did not just yank my tail! she mentally squealed at him.

"I did. And I'm doing it again." Tug.

Such disrespect. He'd pay for it. She narrowed her gaze on him. He laughed and beckoned her before sweeping away. With a trilling cry she couldn't contain, she went after him.

Anger didn't put the fierce smile on her face; the chase, the adrenaline, the pure fun of being outside made her grin—which she should note also resembled the I'm-gonna-shred-and-eat-you face.

Chances to fly free didn't come often, not with all the rules and permissions. This wasn't a flight in the sunlight, but with a quarter-moon shining, and with the stars, it was bright enough to fly.

Wheee. Might as well enjoy it while she could. Mother would freak. Then again, when didn't she freak?

But she'd have more important things to lose her mind about than the fact that Aimi had flown after jumping out of a plane.

The Crimson Sept had moved against them. The question was, had that dragoness worked alone with her wyvern minions, or was this just the beginning of a larger movement?

Whatever the reason, Aimi wouldn't tolerate anyone coming after Brand. *My mate.*

They kept to the higher skies, avoiding the spots of light scattered below. Every so often, they found an uninhabited patch of land, wide fields, and forests. They took a chance and skimmed low across treetops, Brand sometimes awing her with how deep in the woods he'd dip. Brand's hybrid figure could move with sharp grace, his smaller size giving him an intriguing maneuverability.

They flew for hours, some words spoken between them but, for the most part, just hovering close, a comforting camaraderie between them that sometimes turned electric when he would come close and run a finger down her scales. She could feel his admiration. She thrived on it.

Dawn fast approached, and she knew they couldn't fly forever. The lights of a city beckoned over the plains, the arid land they'd traversed giving way to civilization.

She alighted, and after a moment, he joined her. "Why did we stop?"

Because we can't just coast into the city.

"Why not?" He cocked his head.

Because someone will see us.

"Yup. They might. And they might even take a picture that will probably grace the cover of a newspaper with a headline like, 'Dragons are stealing your pets.'"

We do not eat cats and dogs. She couldn't help an indignant reply.

"Then you're missing out." With his expression flat, she couldn't tell if he joked or not.

We should find some clothes.

"Speak for yourself, I have pants."

Not for long if you keep antagonizing me. She bared her teeth, and he laughed.

"You want me naked, then you just need to say the word, moonbeam."

Actually, she did want him naked, but her wishes to do decadent things to his body would have to wait. By now, the plane would have completed an emergency landing—or crashed. Officials would be crawling all over it, checking off the passengers on the list, noting a few were missing.

It might be difficult to explain how she and Brand had survived, but knowing her mother, she'd bribe some official, Adi would fudge some records, and everything would work out. Of more importance, they needed to get to that party with his sister tonight. For that, she needed her human body and clothes.

I'll be back. I need to go shopping. Before he could reply, she took to the skies, and he quickly followed, trailing her as she scouted until she found what she needed. A clothesline. A quick dive and she snared a dress from the line, the pins holding the garment snapping at the hard yank.

Alighting a few hundred yards away, it took her only a moment to change into the oversized dress that had probably once graced a discount rack at a big box store. Her mother would be appalled. How Aimi wished for a camera so she could send her a picture.

She smoothed the skirt down and turned to address Brand, who stood sentinel over her. "Did you have to be such a gentleman?"

"Are you complaining because I respected

you?" The confused look returned, more adorable than ever.

"Would it have killed you to maul me while I was trying to dress?"

"Mauling would have led to other things. We don't have the time, and we are also lacking a bed."

"Where's your sense of adventure?"

"Back on the plane. I've had enough adventure for the moment. I'd take a little bit of quiet now before we dive back into it tonight."

Ah, yes, tonight's mission. They'd rescue his sister, and he'd show his proper appreciation. In bed. "You're right. Time's a wasting. Shall we go hitch ourselves a ride?"

"No riding. I'll fly."

"It's too dangerous. Lots of guns out here, and quick trigger fingers."

"It wouldn't be the first time I was shot."

"Don't make me break your wings."

"Don't make me put you over my knee."

"You do realize that's not a threat."

"I know." He smiled. "And we don't have time for that either right now. We have to get moving."

"Flying won't be enough. And you're tired. We need to hitch a lift."

"In case you hadn't noticed, I'm not exactly hitchhiking material." His wings fluttered.

"America loves green reptiles. Look at Kermit still going strong decades later."

"Kermit can sing. I can't."

"You're right. You can't be a Muppet frog because that would make me a pig. This is probably wrong somehow"—her nose wrinkled—"but I am so craving bacon right now."

"Your mind is a fascinating place."

"So is my bed, so come on, let's go find one." She took a few steps, only to have Brand scoop her into his arms. "What are you doing?"

"Carrying you. In case you hadn't noticed, your feet are bare, and the ground is rough." Chivalry. How adorable.

"Your feet are bare, too."

"But I'm not walking." He flapped his wings and rose, taking her with him. "I'll drop you close to a service station. There's got to be one close by. You should be able to snare a ride from there."

"Not without you, I'm not." She wouldn't let them get separated, especially not after the attack. This was a direct strike against the Silvergrace family. It didn't matter their goal appeared to be Brand, a rival Sept had attacked and tried to steal. That was grounds for war.

Brand is mine. Woe to any dragonesses or their minions who thought to take him. They just had to wait twenty-four hours, maybe less if she got some sleep—not likely with Brand around. In just under a day, she'd have more Dust to unmake her enemies. Which made her wonder if perhaps Aunt Waida had been right when she'd said, "Buy a gun, it's quicker."

"Sorry, moonbeam, but we're going to have to split up. Unless you brought a pearl to flip me back?" She shook her head, and he shrugged. "Then I'm not going to be much good to you. Guess we'll have to devise a new plan for my sister."

"You need to stop being a Debbie Downer." She reached up to rub his cheek, loving the fine-ridged lines. "Haven't you realized you don't need the bead? You obviously have more control than you realize. You managed to shift into your hybrid shape. Now shift out of it."

"I can't."

"You will if you want me to blow you." The dirty promise caused them to dip as his wing strokes faltered for a moment.

He recovered. "You don't play fair."

Nope, she didn't. She nibbled his jawline as she murmured. "My mother always taught me to win by any means necessary."

"And is that all I am, a prize to be won?"

He was more than just a prize, more than the sum of all her treasures. "You are mine."

Softly said, and yet he hugged her tightly, and she felt his pleasure at her words through the bond connecting them. His *need*.

The neon lights of a gas station lit the dark sky, and as promised, he landed before they could illuminate his presence. However, when he placed her on the ground, she turned and grabbed his hands, ignoring the scales covering them and the talons tipping the fingers.

"You're coming with me."

"I can't—"

"You can," she insisted. "Close your eyes and relax. You seem to forget you own this body. You choose its shape. Relax and take control."

He closed his eyes and grimaced. "This is dumb. It won't work. Don't you think I tried and tried to shift at will when I was at Bittech?"

"Perhaps you lacked the right incentive." She leaned forward and lightly pressed her mouth against the hard seam of his lips.

The entire length of his body tensed, and through her bond, she felt panic, shame…longing.

She wound her arms around him and spoke softly against his mouth. "Change for me, Brand. I need a man. My man. I need you."

A shudder went through him, and she loosened her embrace. The second time she kissed him, his lips were as human as hers, but his tongue had a mind of its own as it inserted itself and stroked hers.

His hands palmed her ass as the embrace deepened, and she sighed into his mouth.

Then she almost bit him as he said, "There's a car coming."

Indeed, a Jeep pulled into the service station, the driver a fellow who reeked of weed but who thought nothing of offering them a ride when he heard their friends had ditched them as a prank.

He dropped them at a motel on the outskirts of a major city, and Brand frowned as he looked around.

"This is where you want us to stay for the night?"

"What's wrong with this place?" she asked, cocking her head.

"Because it's the kind of place my family would stay at, not someone like you."

"Are you accusing me of being a snob?"

"Aren't you?"

"I am. I could never stay in a place like this. I mean, really, have you seen the inside of those rooms?" She shuddered. "The carpet requires a good fire cleansing, and there is not enough bleach for those sheets. No dragon should ever sleep in such a pit."

"So if we're not staying here, then why did you have us dropped in this location?"

"Because this is the spot." Lights bobbed at the end of the street, moving quickly along, the engine roaring with a deep V-8 growl she coveted. The dark-tinted muscle car shot past, screeched to a halt, and reversed.

A window rolled down, and a head popped out, sporting silver curls with hints of red. "Is that you, bratface?"

"Hey, Natty." Aimi waved. "That's my cousin," she informed Brand as she dragged him by the hand toward the vehicle. "She's our ride."

He braced himself against her tug to ask, "How did she know to pick us up here?"

"What do you think I was doing with our last driver's phone?"

"I don't know. You called your mom by the sounds of it and didn't say much other than we're all right. You never even mentioned the name of this motel to anyone."

She rolled her eyes. "Of course, I didn't. What if someone was listening in?"

"Says the girl who didn't take her paranoia pill today."

"Seeing as how you're the one who was experimented on and is running from more than a few folks, I'd say you should take lessons from me in staying safe. First lesson, always assume someone is spying."

"Like me," Natty chimed, "and hubby over here. Totally not giving you any privacy on account you're interesting."

"It's not spying if I can see you," he pointed out. "And I am still waiting for an explanation on how your cousin found us if you didn't tell your mom we were here. Is this a setup of some sort? Did you intentionally have the plane attacked and have us fly all night so we'd land here?"

Suspicion clouded his gaze, and she could have beamed in pride. "You just mastered lesson number two. Always assume someone is out to get you."

"Is lesson three the one where I kill all the crazy people?"

"Only if I get to help." Aimi winked. Then laughed. "Just kidding. I only kill if I have to."

"Not entirely reassured."

She leaned forward to whisper, "Have you forgotten I feel what you feel? And right now, I feel how hot you think I am."

"The fact you're sexy doesn't detract from you not telling me everything. How did your cousin know to come here?"

"If you'd been paying attention, then you'd know when I told my mother that we were delayed and thinking of stopping in for a chalupa before renting a car that I was really saying we were safe, on the ground looking for wheels in Flagstaff. All part of the contingency plan."

"A contingency plan that assumed the plane would crash?"

"First off, I doubt the plane crashed." Her twin bond to Adi still held strong, and the adrenaline in it had given way to irritation, which usually meant Adi was dealing with paperwork and idiots. "Second, have you already forgotten your second lesson?

People are always out to kill us. Humans or dragons. It doesn't matter who we prepare for. Our kind didn't survive this long by not planning for every possibility, and that includes having to bail on the flight." Ever since their father's fiery demise, Mother never let them fly without going over Plan B, C, and D. "We have rendezvous points pre-set up around the world, especially here in the States."

"Still, though, we just got here, and we didn't even have to wait for our ride. Your cousin just happened along right after."

"The tracking chip probably helped with the timing."

"You're wearing a GPS?"

"Yup." She grinned before swinging into the back seat of the car. "And so are you."

"You microchipped me like a dog?" he bellowed, and quite indignantly, too.

So she popped her head out to add, "And you might have gotten a few shots to ensure you were germ-free, too, while you were passed out. You'll be glad to know you're protected from every known disease to man and dragon now, including ticks and fleas."

"Does anyone have anything to protect me from crazy women?" he grumbled, and yet a glowering Brand joined her in the vehicle.

Curls bobbing, Natty turned around in the front seat to peek at them while her husband, Sam, put the car in gear and shot off again.

"Nice duds," Natty snickered.

Tugging at the fabric, Aimi grimaced. "I could have done without the flowers and stripes. But I don't want to talk about my new fashion statement.

What happened to the plane I was on? Did it land all right?"

"Were you on the plane that went down?" Her eyes widened. "Shoot, no one told me that. I was just told to get my ass to the motel and do a pickup."

"So there's news then about the flight?"

"Only public stuff so far. According to the media, some plane had to make an emergency landing in the middle of bumfuck due to mechanical failure."

"If by 'mechanical failure' you mean the gaping holes in its side on account we were attacked, then yes."

"No way!" Natty's eyes widened. "Who did it?"

"Wyverns led by a red dragon."

"They wouldn't dare attack. It would start a war."

"Oh, it will, and they might not be the only ones to try. The Silver Sept has recently added something of possibly incredible value to the hoard."

"What?" Natty couldn't help the avarice that shone in her eyes. No dragon could.

"I can't say yet. All in due time. Meanwhile, you haven't met my mate yet. Brand Mercer, meet my cousin, Natalia Silvercrest. And that's her husband, Samuel. His brother, Leopold, is married to my older sister, Mika."

"Apparently, the fact that our families are married doesn't mean shit. How did you get mated without me hearing about it or being invited to the party?" Natty glowered and pouted at the same time.

"It happened suddenly—"

"As in like a day ago," he muttered.

"And it's not official yet." Something she really needed to rectify now that there was attention being turned his way.

"What Sept is he from? I don't recognize him." Natty leaned closer and sniffed. "He's not silver."

"You'll never guess his color."

"Because I don't have one. I'm not a dragon." Silly man just couldn't admit it. Probably a good thing for the moment.

"What does he mean he's not a dragon?" Natty took a longer inhalation to truly absorb his scent. "That definitely smells like dragon. Honey"— she turned to look at Sam—"you've got a good nose, what does he smell like to you?"

"Dragon. But I don't know his Sept either."

"What color is he?" Natty's head cocked as she perused Brand, who simply shook his head and muttered a low, "The crazy gene lives on in all of them."

"His color is a surprise." The biggest surprise. "And you'll learn about it at the reception we're going to have to celebrate our joining. So keep an eye open for an invite."

At her side, he grumbled. "You're assuming a lot of things, moonbeam."

"Assumptions are for those who don't know the truth." She turned to snare his gaze. "I know everything I need to know about you." *You are mine.*

And was it her, or did he finally have his emotions shuttered enough that all she heard was, *Ditto.*

"Sounds as if you have an interesting courtship to relate. I can't wait to hear all about it."

Cousin Natty might have managed to hide her envy in her speech but couldn't exactly conceal the coveting in her eyes. Poor Natty might care for her husband, but theirs was an arranged marriage. They were just lucky it worked out.

"I promise to spill the details as soon as I can over at least two bottles of Mother's finest. Now, enough about Brand and me. I need more news on my sister and cousins. Do you have a phone I can borrow?"

A bedazzled smartphone appeared. Pretty. She snared it and might have stroked the real diamonds glued to it before dialing. The phone was answered on the second ring.

"Rim jobs for five dollars." Her sister uttered it with the grace of a professional barker and then snickered. "How's it going, sis? I see Natty found you."

"Nice to see you're alive and not a meat pie. Did everyone else make it, too?" Because when she'd called her mother, they were still trying to get proper details.

"The girls and I all made it, most of the other passengers, too, but there was a bunch of boys on the plane... Yeah, they should have buckled their belts. So tragic." Snicker. "Not."

"Are we clear?" Aimi asked.

"You can talk. I've secured the line."

"What are the surviving passengers saying?"

"They were all passed out from the pressure by the time the plane landed." And those that weren't, probably got a sharp rap to the noggin. "When they regained consciousness, they tried to blab about monsters and dragons. Odd how the cousins and I saw sharks and snakes. Officials are dismissing our recollection of events as hallucinations caused by the depressurization of the cabin."

"And the pilots?"

"Saw nothing."

"So what's the status on those missing? Are they looking for bodies?" In other words, were they sure the wyverns had died? She knew the dragoness had, but that still left her accomplices.

"It's doubtful any survived a fall from that high. Since officials can't be sure where the bodies landed, they're just putting out a general notice to law enforcement to be on the lookout along the flight path of the plane for heaps of meat."

"Any more news?"

"Yes, there's a stewardess from our flight currently on suspension given she missed the fact that two of her passengers went missing before takeoff. It's truly incompetent how our flight attendant didn't notice you and Speedy arguing as you left the plane before she sealed the flight deck."

"So we're in the clear?"

"As possible. We played with their computers a bit. The paperwork for the headcount is missing, and the airline staff is frazzled. Add in our story of events, and you should be fine. Listen, I got to go. There's a cute cop I want to have interrogate me again."

No surprise there. Her sister had a thing for handcuffs.

"See you at the hotel, then?" Aimi asked.

"Not likely. I don't see any of us arriving anytime soon. We landed in the middle of tweedle-fucking-dumville. They have got the tiniest airport in existence, currently shut down because it's under FAA jurisdiction while they investigate the cause of the plane's demise. Which means, no flying out."

"So drive."

"Gee, wish I'd thought of it." Her sister's voice oozed sarcasm. "The town has got like…nothing. No taxi service or car rental. They've got us in a community center waiting for a shuttle bus to come. But that is going to take hours."

"Not the way Deka drives. Get her to bribe the driver. You could probably still make it."

"Not going to happen. So enjoy a night off, and we'll come up with something new when we get there."

"I can't wait that long." Impatience wasn't something she enjoyed dealing with.

"Don't you dare go to that party without us."

"Then you'd better hope that bus grows wing and gets your ass here fast because we are going to that party." The sooner she got Brand's little sister, the sooner she could claim him. Although, she had to admit, the spot of danger proved exciting. Would mating stop the Septs from coming after him?

I hope not. Boredom belonged to those who didn't truly live.

She hung up and handed the phone back to her cousin. "How far can you take us?"

"Where you going?"

"Beverly Hills."

"We can hit an airfield I know and borrow a Cessna. We'd be there in just over two hours. Or we can drive all the way, which is like eight."

She winced. "Ouch. I think we should—"

"Drive," Brandon stated, echoed a second

later by Sam.

"But it will take so long." She might have pouted as she said it.

"It might be longer, but what are the chances we'll be attacked on the road versus the sky?"

"It's almost sunrise. Dragons don't fly in the day."

"I'll bet they're not supposed to attack planes either, and yet, look what happened."

Sam merged onto a highway, and the car put on even more speed. "By car, we can evade them better. They might know where we're going, but not how we're getting there."

"Unless they've got really good spies and are detecting our locator signals." As soon as she uttered it, Aimi longed for some tinfoil. She also had a revelation.

No wonder Aunt Waida says wear metal panties if you don't want them watching you. Did it disrupt the signal?

"Do you really think they'll come after you again? I mean you are in Silvercrest territory. They wouldn't dare." Natty held her chin high in pride. Cute that she stuck up for her family, and yet, it turned out she was wrong.

Apparently, some families would dare once they passed the Silvercrest land boundary into no man's land. Their attackers waited until a barren stretch, the sun mid-morning high, and everyone in the car partially drowsing except for Sam.

Good thing, because when a vehicle came shooting out of nowhere, he swerved the car hard enough to give them whiplash but avoided a collision. Rubber squealed, and gravel flew in a dusty cloud behind them as the tires of the car looked to regain traction. He hit the pavement, and the car shot like a dragon out of a volcano—which was way faster than a bat out of hell according to one of her great aunts.

"What the fuck just happened?" Natty bolted upright and slapped her hands on the dash, checking things out around them.

"We have company." Understatement of the year went to Sam.

From behind, a car chased. Ahead of them, they could see another heading straight on.

But the truly crowning moment was the pair of shadows overhead.

Dragons. In daylight. Holy fuck. Even her mother would be too stunned to make her gargle castor oil now.

Brand tensed beside her. "We're under attack again."

"We should have stopped for tinfoil," she muttered, turning around to peer at the car hugging their tail.

"How would tinfoil help?"

"Jamming signals. We just had the spy question answered. Someone has access to our GPS signal, and I do believe another family has just declared war." Because those were yellows in the sky. "We might want to duck. One of the guys in the car behind us has a gun."

Her remark was met a moment later by the cracking of glass as a slug hit the rear window and spiderwebbed it.

"My car. He hit my car." Sam's voice rose in pitch. He slammed the brakes, and the abrupt stop caused the car behind to swerve on the road, unwilling to crash into them.

Sam reached under his seat before opening his door and stepping out.

"Does he have a gun?" Brand asked.

"Under every seat," Natty admitted, head popping up along with the muzzle of a rifle. "You wouldn't believe how many he has stashed in the house. He's a huge fan of *The Walking Dead*."

Crack. Crack. Bullets peppered the area as Sam braced his AK-47 and sprayed it across the car that braked behind them and then flipped around to Swiss cheese the one trying to reverse.

As for the shadows overhead, Natty angled back and took aim. A squawk of pain met one shot, but the dragons were smart. As soon as they'd noted the guns coming out, they took to higher skies. In moments, the attack was thwarted with no casualty— but the car—on their side.

As they stood leaning against the vehicle, Sam paid a visit to the two vehicles and made sure, after wiping it down for prints, to place his gun with one of them. Then he placed an identical one with the other shooter, covering his tracks.

"Let's go." Sam swung into the car, cool as a glacier in the arctic, and Natty bounced in beside him.

"I don't suppose there is any point in insisting it's getting too dangerous, and I should go on alone?" Brand eyed them and the wrecks.

"If you're going to be mated to Aimi, then that makes you family."

"Get in," said Sam, then, in a very Terminator style, put on some glasses and added, "They'll be back."

A pity they had a party to go to or Aimi would have waited for them.

As it was, they did have to stop for tinfoil. She didn't know if it stopped them from emitting a signal, but she sure enjoyed helping Brand craft one for his groin, even if he ruined her fun by not allowing her to make it anatomically correct.

Chapter Thirteen

The rest of the trip went off without any attacks. Brand wasn't entirely sure they had the aluminum foil to thank but more the fact that they soon entered more civilized areas with people watching.

The dragons might have launched some brazen attacks but thus far had done so only in secluded locations where discovery seemed unlikely.

Did he believe for a moment he was safe?

Nope, which meant Aimi wasn't safe either because the damnable woman wouldn't abandon him. She didn't seem to grasp that being with him equaled danger. Actually, that wasn't entirely true. She understood, she just didn't seem to care, and a part of her seemed to thrive on it. He could feel it through their link, the excitement, and the cold determination. Cute and ladylike on the outside didn't mean shit. Inside lurked someone who wouldn't hesitate to act.

So fucking sexy. Brandon never thought himself a guy to get turned on by a woman undaunted by anything, even violence, but that was before he'd met his moonbeam.

My moonbeam. And he planned to keep it that way, despite not knowing how that would work. He remained convinced he wasn't good enough for her, not by a long shot. However, he also couldn't bring himself to walk away. The selfish Mercer genes at play. It wasn't just dragons who liked to hoard pretty things, especially valuable things they shouldn't have.

The hotel they were booked to stay at was a gorgeous Marriott, considered a neutral zone by the Septs for this region. These neutral lodgings were scattered around the world, part of the treaties all dragons supposedly abided by to ensure they could vacation and deal with business interests. The only thing expected when dragons arrived onto another's territory was that they notify the local family Sept of their arrival.

"Isn't giving your enemy a copy of your itinerary counterproductive?" he'd asked when Aimi explained it to him.

"Dragons don't kill dragons." When he raised a brow, she added, "Often. We have to be severely provoked to move against our kind."

"Provoked such as the attack on our plane?"

"Yes. I've never heard of anything so brazen. Most times, we deal with issues in a civilized manner."

"What do you call civilized?"

A wide grin showed sharp white teeth—*teeth that should be nibbling my skin.* "Cooperate takeovers. Attacks on their stocks. Tabloids stories."

'But doesn't that make your enemies madder and even more out for revenge?"

She'd blinked. "Well, yeah. That's the whole point."

Such a different world he'd entered. In the bayou, arguments were usually solved with a few punches, and for the really heinous shit, the bayou left no evidence—and neither did his aunt with her recently published cookbook, *Trap 'Em and Eat 'Em, the swamp guide to cooking critters without wasting any parts*."

It wasn't selling enough to hit any bestseller lists, but Aunt Tanya became an instant celebrity among the Mercers and other swamp folk.

Brandon felt dirty and underdressed when Sam pulled under the canopy for the hotel. Before they piled out of the car, Natty turned in her seat.

"Here's some cash and a credit card." A silver card, not black as he would have expected.

"Where are you going?" Brandon asked.

"Back home," Natty replied. "If the reds are massing for an assault, then we need to prepare."

"I think you're safe," Aimi announced, slipping the flip-flops they'd bought at a gas station on her feet. "They're after Brand. But they're not getting him."

Mine. The word practically sang between them, and the cold in him warmed with a strange iciness at odds with the emotion.

The shoes weren't the only things they'd grabbed at the gas station. A prepaid cell phone that wouldn't leave a trace, a T-shirt for him with a reptile sunning itself on the front with the caption, "Wanna pet my lizard?"

He and Aimi piled out of the car with the taped-cardboard back window and watched it pull away.

The front desk didn't bat an eyelid at their strange outfits.

As for Aimi, she acted as if she wore designer

duds and perfectly coiffed hair. "A suite please, with a balcony facing the front, top floor." Paying cash meant she could sign in with any name she liked. She chose Mr. and Mrs. Silvergrace.

He didn't say anything about it until they'd entered the elevator.

"Silvergrace? You do realize if you're serious about claiming me, then you'll have to take my name. Mercer."

"If I'm serious?" Her lips curved. "You should know by now I mean what I say."

He did know, and she needed to learn she wouldn't be calling all the shots. "I think Mrs. Mercer has a nice ring to it. Don't you?"

"It's not a dragon name."

"I'm not a dragon." He penned her with his arms, letting the bulk of his body pin her against the wall as the numbers to the floors flashed. "I say you'll take whatever name I tell you."

"Are you giving me orders?" Her query emerged with a hint of irritation—but she also couldn't hide arousal as he finally asserted his desires.

"I'm telling you how it's going to be, moonbeam." Before she could retort, the elevator stopped, and there was a ding as the doors slid open.

He stepped out and strode to one of the few doors on this level. The keycard switched the red light to green, and he entered.

Hot damn, now this is what I call swanky accommodations.

The room she'd booked proved lavish, so lavish that, when he stepped in, he almost turned right back around. These weren't the kind of digs he usually stayed in.

I am definitely not the kind of guy who should be staying somewhere like this.

"Chin up, shoulders back. You do belong."

"Was I thinking aloud again?" He'd been trying to control his mental yelling.

"It was your expression that gave it away. Actually, you've been good about keeping your thoughts to yourself. A shame, I miss the dirty ones." She winked, and he couldn't help it. The dirtiest thought crossed his mind involving her on her knees, lips wrapped around a certain part of him, her sultry expression peering upward.

Her lips rounded, and arousal flickered between them, a fire ready to consume. He took a step toward her, only to have her turn away as she kicked off the plastic flip-flops and sank her dirty toes into the carpet.

"I need a shower," she declared.

Would a tongue bath work instead? He was so sure he'd kept that raunchy comment locked down, and yet she tossed him a saucy grin over her shoulder. "I'll leave the door open in case you need me. Whatever you do, don't answer the door. If someone knocks, ignore it."

"Giving me orders again?"

"Just giving you chances to disobey. But do try not to get killed. I'd prefer to ravage, not avenge, you."

"Ravage, right." His saucy moonbeam took her pert ass out of sight, and he eyed the door out of the suite.

He could leave, right this instant. Open that door and just go. It would be best. Safer for Aimi, her family, everyone who came in contact with him.

The attack on the road proved that the invasion on the plane wasn't a one-time thing.

People are after me. And they didn't care who they hurt.

All because they think I'm a dragon. Some kind of noble gold one. As if. The only things running through his veins were swamp sludge and the Mercer curse.

He took a step toward the door then another. His hand touched the knob, and he stopped.

Can I really abandon her like this? Without a word? It sounded cowardly, and yet, he knew if he told her of his departure, she'd convince him to stay because she wanted him.

No matter how he tried to convince her otherwise, the damned woman wanted to claim him.

He turned the knob and, through their bond, quite clearly heard, *I will chase your ass down if you walk out that door, and I don't care if I'm naked and wet while doing it.*

Naked and wet. He might have gone blind and stupid for a second as his mind filled with that image.

Slam. *Click.* He deadbolted the door and, before he could finish his blink, found himself standing in the doorway for the bathroom.

Steam enveloped him, the warm, damp tendrils wrapping and teasing, obscuring even further Aimi's naked body behind the frosted glass of the shower.

"I see you decided to stay." She peeked around the edge of the enclosure. "Our family lawyer thanks you. We just had the ban lifted from our last little incident."

"Dare I ask for what?"

"Let's just say that some people have way too much imagination and not enough sense of humor when it comes to olive oil, goats, and rubber gloves."

"You do realize it would be safer for you to let me go. I know how to disappear."

"Not from me you can't." Again she glanced out at him, her features damp and hair slicked back. "That connection between us won't break that easily and will only get stronger when I fully claim you."

"*If* you claim me. I'm not the dragon you're looking for."

"No, you're not. I was looking for someone malleable and simple-minded." She shut off the water and stepped out of the shower, not hiding her body at all. It never failed to draw his eye. The beautiful slim lines of it with a hint of a curve at the hip, more at the breast, the toned length of her thigh. "I thought what I wanted was a puppet that I could pull out and play with at will. Then I found you."

"So you settled for a low-born, desperate man with a price on his head to thwart your mother and get you out of the house."

"All true, except for the part where I settled. Meeting you made me realize that what I want and what I need isn't the same thing. I need to feel alive. I want a partner. With you, I get that and so much more."

"Like possible eviction from your family if it turns out I'm not dragon. I've heard enough, moonbeam, in the last two days to know that dragons take their bloodlines super serious."

"They do." She stepped closer, eschewing the towel. "But do you know what I take more seriously?" Closer. Whispered. "Me. Because"—she gripped his shirt and lifted on tiptoe to growl—"the world revolves around me, and in my world, I deserve happiness. So get over yourself and get with the program." She nipped his chin. He almost dropped to the floor to worship her.

Then he found his balls. Pretty words wouldn't change who he was.

Bang. Bang. Bang. "Room service."

"I didn't order anything." She frowned.

"Me either. Coming," he hollered.

He ignored her hissed, "I told you not to open the door," and headed to the portal. A peek through the hole showed a fisheye view of a hotel employee, a tray on wheels at his side.

"I think you have the wrong room," he mentioned.

The guy wearing a collared shirt with a nametag pinned to it shrugged and replied, "Compliments of management and a courtesy offered to all our cherished higher-tier guests."

So this was the kind of service that came with the big bucks. Cool. Especially since he was hungry.

The bathroom door closed behind Aimi, hiding her delectable shape. Brand unlocked the room door, opened it, and gestured for the guy to come in. The fellow no sooner walked past than his senses tingled.

Danger. He released the door and caught the guy in a headlock, his foot sweeping at ankles and taking him down. He pinned the guy with an arm across the throat and leaned down close, the cold within him pushing.

"Who sent you?"

"Hotel. Food." Fingers clawed at his arm, and

wide eyes pled for mercy. But the chill within him ignored it.

He lies.

Brand pressed harder on his windpipe. "Who. Sent. You?" The determined tone of his words froze the guy. He stopped struggling, and his features went flat. "I am but a cog in the machine that is the order of gold."

"What is the order of gold?"

"It's a silly sect that believes if a gold dragon returns so shall our freedom, and that we shall rule the world again." Aimi was the one to reply, stepping from the bathroom, hints of moisture still clinging to her skin, most of her hidden—a shame—in a complimentary robe.

What a pity it hides her from my gaze. Then again, none should look upon her but me. His shiny thing, and no one else's.

"Don't tell me. I'm supposed to be this dragon?" He snorted and removed his arm from the guy. "You are all so fucking nuts and mistaken."

"As the last golden dragon, you need to come with me," insisted the guy, sitting up, unperturbed at all by how close he'd come to dying. "We are ready to fly by your side in the coming battle."

Someone needed to chug some meds. "Get out and tell whoever you're working with to stop their attempts. I'm not a gold dragon. I'm not a dragon at all."

"The portents all say the return of the king is imminent. The order of gold only wishes to protect you."

"Protect me by attacking?"

"I was not sent to attack but retrieve."

"Alone?" Aimi frowned. "Why would they only send one minion? And a puny one at that?"

"Who says I'm alone?" There was a pause after he'd spoken. "Anytime now!" Brandon's captive hollered.

Again, nothing happened.

Aimi snickered. "Did you think we chose this hotel by chance?"

"I thought you chose it because it's some kind of neutral zone," Brand replied.

"It is, but it's also had its security overhauled recently with some really high-tech shit. Given I used the Silvergrace name, you can bet that immediately raised a flag in their system, putting them on high alert. Which means they took steps to ensure their guests, in this case, me, wouldn't be disturbed. I'll bet whoever else they sent got snared by security."

"I am less than impressed." Brand grabbed the fellow by the shirt and hauled him to his feet before giving him a little shake. "I think they missed a pretty obvious intruder."

"More like allowed him through that we might question him."

"Now that he's answered, what are we supposed to do with him?"

"I am feeling a little peckish." She eyed the guy with a feral smile.

The only man she's eating is me. "I'm more keen on eating what's under those domes than his stringy carcass."

"Spoilsport. Then again, I did just shower. I suppose we'll just have to hold on to him for security."

"What about the backup he was expecting?"

"Probably already in custody. The Septs won't be happy that this group thought to break the neutral accord. I expect they, and whichever Sept is behind them, will be punished."

"I would never betray my brothers and sisters! Glory to the gold." With that shout, the guy broke from Brand's grasp and ran for the patio doors. It took but a moment for him to yank them open. Brand dashed after him, only to arrive in time to see their intruder dive off the balcony, arms spread.

He didn't fall far as he hit some kind of invisible barrier that vaporized him.

Puff. Dust filtered down.

Brand gaped. "What the fuck just happened?"

"I told you the hotel had a good security system."

"Security doesn't just eliminate people in a second flat. That kind of technology doesn't exist." He turned around and saw her through the open patio door.

She snorted. "It has existed for years. It's just not in use where the public knows about it."

"You know about it."

"Because I'm special. Now, are you going to stand around in those dirty duds all day, or are you going to make use of that shower?"

"I'm a little more concerned right now about the fact that we've got enemies who know where we are and keep coming after us."

"Exciting, isn't it? But given how catastrophically they just failed, I doubt we'll see any more action while we're at the hotel. So why don't you shower while I see if I can wrangle us some clothes and information?"

"We have food." He pointed to the tray.

"Which is more than likely drugged. I'll order us something fresh. Unless you'd like to dine in." The less-than-subtle finger dragged down the vee left by the robe.

Hell yes, I'd like to eat her. It just wasn't the smart thing to do right now. Too many loose ends meant he had to decide on which to focus on first. As exciting as bedding Aimi would be, he couldn't get distracted from his prime reason for being here.

His sister. The thought of her acted as a damper on his ardor, and so he went for that shower, but no matter how cold the water, his blood ran hot.

So hot.

And throbbing, mustn't forget the throbbing.

It had been so long since he was a man, a real man with soft flesh, not scales, that now it felt strange to grip himself. To feel his turgid length. He could feel the calluses on his hands—working hands as the girls called them—as he stroked the length of himself.

The water in the shower and the soap made it easy to glide back and forth along the length. Squeezing. Pumping.

As his breath grew ragged, vivid fantasies rolled like a movie inside his head: Aimi on her back for him, her thighs spread, showing off the pink folds of her pussy.

He could still recall the titillating taste of her nipples in his mouth. The sound of her soft sighs and moans as he fingered her.

The reminder of how she'd climaxed, back arched, mouth open wide in a silent cry, the muscles of her channel gripping him so tight. His hips thrust as his hand stroked. Caught in his fantasy, he could almost imagine she was with him, encouraging him— *Faster*—welcoming him—*Deeper.*

Coming with him. *Mark me.*

How disappointing to open his eyes and realize he was alone.

But it was for the best. He still hadn't changed his mind. Aimi deserved better than him. So much better. What could he offer her? He didn't have a job or a home. Hell, he didn't even have any clothes anymore to call his own.

What did he bring to the table?

Himself? *Talk about her getting gypped.*

Chapter Fourteen

I feel so gypped. He didn't even try to cajole her into joining him for a shower. Then again, she would have had to say no. She had matters to attend.

As soon as Brand closed the door and locked it—so cute, especially since she could bust that door off its hinges any time she wanted—she dove on her temporary cell phone.

A quick dial was answered with a no-nonsense, "What happened? Our accounting firm just pinged me to inform us we've been billed for an incident at the hotel in Beverly Hills."

"Whatever happened to the love, Mother? Like, hi, Aimi, are you okay?"

"You're obviously fine; you called me. As for love, you know I don't believe in mollycoddling." No, Mother didn't. However, despite Aimi's bitching, she knew her mother cared. Had something happened to Aimi, or her sister, there was nothing and no one that would be safe from her mother's wrath.

Tiger and soccer moms had nothing on dragon ones.

"We had some unexpected guests show up at the hotel, from that religion you were telling me about. The ones who believe in a gold savior. They are after Brand."

"How did they know about him?" Immediately followed by a terse, "We have a leak." Aimi could practically see the cold steam rising from her mother even through the phone.

"Or a hacker." Adi was always going on about how nothing was safe anymore. Encryption was just a fancy word for a difficult puzzle. But all puzzles had a solution; some just took longer to crack.

"I will deal with whoever is leaking our secrets. Given the breach, you are to stay in that hotel room with the possible gold until your sister and cousins arrive."

"Which is when?"

"Tomorrow."

"Too late. The party is tonight."

"Then you'll have to postpone."

"And miss a chance to get into Parker's place? Not likely."

"Are you disobeying me, *child*?" Spoken in a tone meant to put Aimi in her place.

"Every chance I get, Mother."

Laughter met her reply. "So headstrong. Reminds me of someone I know, and exactly what I'd expect of my daughter. Very well, if you insist on doing this, then be smart. I will do what I can from my end to ensure you have support, but you might not necessarily recognize it. Suspect everyone, and only start a war if you have to."

"Who, me?" Said with just the right hint of innocence.

"I'm serious, Aimi." Her mother's voice became completely resolute. "We are at a dangerous threshold in our existence. There have been too many reports lately of big birds in the sky. Speculation is one thing, but should the humans realize we are among them, we stand to lose much."

"So you keep saying, but at some point, we won't be able to hide. The world has changed too much for that."

"Then maybe we'll just have to change it back."

Short of a massive electromagnetic pulse and a destruction of the world's factories, technology was here to stay. "Good luck shoving that cat back in the bag."

"It's easier than you'd think once you wring its neck. Be careful."

Probably the closest thing Aimi would get to an "I love you," and she didn't like it because it revealed just how worried her mother was. She might act cold and blasé about the situation. However, the rashness of the Crimson Sept, the fact that some fanatics were after Brand, and they didn't know what to expect from this party tonight meant that Aimi needed a killer dress—and even sweeter heels.

She spent the next few minutes arranging them while Brand took a long shower—a dirty one that he couldn't quite hide from her through their link. She almost stalked in after him when she realized what he did in there—naughty boy—but she didn't for two reasons. One, he thought of her to pleasure himself, and two, by relieving some pressure, he'd have more stamina for the real thing. A thing that she needed more than ever.

Before, she'd wanted to claim him to escape her plight with her Sept when she turned twenty-eight—artificial insemination chosen at random from the donated sperm of an adult male dragon wasn't something she aspired to.

Then she wanted to claim him because of who he was, and before anyone else could. *A gold treasure for my hoard.*

Now, she just wanted to claim him because she liked him. *He's mine. All mine, and I'm tired of waiting.*

When he'd exited the shower, he found her splayed on the bed.

"Hello," she said in her most husky tone.

"Did the food arrive yet?"

"It's on its way, along with our clothes for the evening, but it will be about an hour. Plenty of time to indulge in other things." Her fingers dragged down the seam of her robe, tugging it apart. Screw subtlety.

He averted his gaze, for a second, but his eyes returned to stare at the revealed cleavage. "We shouldn't be doing this."

"Why not? I told you the hotel has us secured, and unless you're really bad at it, we won't need that full hour. At least, I won't." She licked her lips.

And still, he rejected her. "I'm not a boy-toy that you can order around. I've told you once, and I'm telling you again, we don't belong together."

She pushed herself to a seated position and fixed him with a hard stare. "We do belong together. So accept it."

"Or what? You'll claim me by force. You know that won't go well if you do."

"Why must you make this so difficult?"

"Why can't you listen? I'm not fit to be your mate. Not you, not anyone. Only a few days ago, I was a hunted monster, a freak of science. Now, I might look like a man, but inside, I'm a fucking mess. My gator has mutated into someone I don't recognize. I don't recognize myself half the time. My thoughts, my perspective, everything about me has changed. And is still changing."

"Because you keep refusing to accept what you are. Once you ascend—"

"Don't you fucking get it? Listen to me, for fuck's sake. I am not a goddamned dragon. I am never going to fucking ascend, so this stubborn insistence that I am some long-lost gold dragon and that I am your perfect mate isn't going to wash. I am a swamp gator. A nothing who doesn't deserve to be in the same room as you, let alone touching you."

The saddest thing about his speech? Through their bond, she could tell he truly believed that. He truly thought himself unworthy of her. That very nobility only served to make her desire for him grow.

She came off the bed and dropped her robe as she did, revealing herself to him in the only way she could.

"I am not unattainable. I am flesh and blood just like you." She grabbed his hand and placed it above her heart. "I won't lie and say I understand exactly what you are, but I can state with certainty that I do want you. Now. I don't care if you're a dragon. Or a pauper. Or even a criminal. It is the man I'm falling for. The man I desire." She slid his hand down her body, pressing it against her mound and noting the slight tic on his face as he felt the heat of her pulsing. "We don't know what will happen tonight." Victory if she had a say. "We don't know what will happen tomorrow." A victory celebration, hello. "But we do have now. This moment. Which is now less than an hour because you keep talking about your feelings when you should know by now—"

"The world revolves around you." Laughter barked out of him, but he didn't pull his hand away. "You are unlike any woman I've known. More stubborn, too."

"I don't know about that. Seems to me I am looking at someone even more thick-headed than me, given I'm still standing here unmolested."

"You want me to fuck you?" He said the crude words as he grabbed her and pulled her tight against him.

"I want to feel you inside me." The truth, and he heard it. She made sure he did through their bond.

"God help me, I want to sink into you. But I can't. I can't have you claim me or make any promises until the situation with my sister and uncle is resolved."

"So we'll just have sex."

"Just?"

"Have incredibly awesome sex." She twined her arms around his neck and drew him down for a kiss. "Don't make me beg."

"Or what?"

"Don't say I didn't warn you." She dropped to her knees and tugged the towel around his hips loose.

There was no hiding his hard shaft. It immediately jutted forth, proud and long and thick. So very thick.

She wrapped a hand around the base of him as he uttered a strangled, "What are you doing?"

"Making you beg." She took the mushroom tip of him into her mouth and sucked.

His answer was a groan and a tremble. She leaned back and conducted a frank appraisal of his body, the lean muscles that started broad in his shoulder, thick in his arms, tapered at his waist. The washboard abs flowed into a vee that led to the prize. He had very little hair around his cock, but that wasn't why he appeared so large. He was just plain big.

"Why are you staring?" he asked in a soft whisper.

"Because I like looking at you." She did. He fascinated her more than all the fine art she'd accumulated thus far in her life.

Her words made his cock grow, and a vein in it pulsed. She adjusted her grip and stroked him up and down.

The engorged tip blushed a deep rose color. Yummy. Aimi dipped forward and flicked her tongue against the swollen head, swirled it around and tasted a drop of his essence.

He let out a loud groan. A good start; however, the ultimate plan involved his complete surrender.

The tip of her tongue bathed his cock, licking all over, making it wet before she took him into her mouth. Open wide, really wide because his girth required room, and it proved a tight fit. He gasped as the edges of her teeth grazed his skin.

Through their link, she could feel his pleasure. It excited her. She could understand now how he'd lost control earlier. By touching him, by pleasing him, she, in turn, got some of it back through their bond.

It aroused her.

No wonder he enjoyed it so much. Would she come as well if he did? Only one way to find out. With her hand gripping the base of his cock, she worked him, up and down, her lips and teeth sliding, her cheeks hollowed as she suctioned.

Her free hand cupped his heavy sac, fondling and kneading, causing a burst of extra-sensory delight.

"Aimi." He whispered her name, aloud or in her head, it didn't matter. Only pleasing him mattered. She squeezed his balls and sucked hard, causing his hips to thrust.

Faster, and faster, Aimi worked his shaft.

"Stop." He said it, and yet he didn't push her away. She knew what he wanted, to sink his cock into her. She wanted it, too.

Through their link, she showed him what she wanted. As she continued to suck, she sent him an image of her positioned over his shaft, rubbing the swollen head against her flesh.

"Aimi." The word was a plea, and she ate him even more hungrily as she imagined herself impaling herself hard on his length, taking him deep into her. He would fill her so tightly. So perfectly. So…

He turned the tables on her and began projecting thoughts of his own. He built upon her fantasy by showing her his hands on her hips, moving her atop him. Pushing her down so he could fill her even more deeply.

In his fantasy, his thumb found her button and rubbed, even as he pulled her forward that his mouth might latch onto the tip of a breast.

She was on the brink of coming. But she held

on. Held on because, dammit, she wanted what he offered.

He dragged her to her feet, her lips swollen, all of her throbbing.

"Take me," she begged. Funny how she'd set out to teach him a lesson but now needed him to teach her one instead.

"Bend over for me."

He growled the words, and she didn't argue. Simply whirled and bent at the waist, presenting herself to him. He roughly curled an arm around her, drawing her back against him, trapping his cock against the crack of her ass. She wiggled against him and made a mewling sound that turned into a sharp cry as he found her clitoris and rubbed it.

"Brand." She sobbed his name as he stroked her.

Then screamed, "Go away!" as someone dared to knock.

She was so close to coming. So close to the treasured climax. How dare someone interrupt.

I shall eat them for their temerity. Stomp them until they are but dust.

She stalked to the hotel door in a high dudgeon, only to have Brand loop his arms around her waist and lift her off the floor. "You can't answer the door naked."

"Yes, I can."

"No, you can't, because then I'd have to murder someone. Put your robe on and behave," he growled before setting her down behind him and giving her a swat on the ass.

He spanked me!

As she gaped at him, he shouted, "Who is it?"

"Room service," was the faint reply.

"Food?" He turned and tossed her a devastating grin. "Excellent, because I'm *hungry.*"

Chapter Fifteen

Yes, it was incredibly naughty of him to leave her hanging and to actually dine on the real food instead of what he wanted: her.

However, moonbeam would have to understand he wouldn't be forced, or seduced, into doing what she wanted, even if he wanted it, too.

He'd almost forgotten all his promises and vows when she blew him—*Am I insane to say no to the woman who drops to her knees and gives me such pleasure?* In that moment, the world, hell, the entire universe, revolved around Aimi. If she'd asked him right then and there, he might have caved to her demands.

Even now with her glowering across from him, a part of him still wanted to give her what she wanted. *She is my everything.* However, making her the center of his universe meant protecting her, sometimes from herself.

Until the situation with his family was resolved, he couldn't let her do something irrevocable, such as permanently claim him. Just like he couldn't let her come with him to this party tonight.

I've already put her in enough danger already. He wouldn't drag her into any more. When she went to the bathroom to douse her girl bits with cold water—

Because someone is a cruel bastard who is asking for me to rip off his balls—-he mixed some of the supposedly drugged food from earlier with the current offering.

Since he couldn't be sure what was drugged and what wasn't, he swapped the iced tea that came in the first cart and switched the fruit plates.

When Aimi exited the bedroom, he was already eating the untainted version.

He ignored her glare. Harder to ignore was her sitting across from him wearing only a robe. It didn't help that he could now picture what hid underneath. Her body was a hell of a lot more appetizing than the filet mignon drizzled with butter he currently savored.

"I can't believe I got ditched for food this time," she grumbled.

"Got to keep my strength up," he teased.

"You're mean."

"Poor, moonbeam. Do you need me to kiss it better?"

"Yes."

"Later. If this mission succeeds." A false hope for them both because, even if he saved his sister, the truth remained: *I am still a Mercer.*

"You are being awfully close-minded," she remarked in between bites.

"I am learning how to control my thoughts. Could come in handy tonight."

"I already told you, it's our special bond that allows me to read you."

"Which I don't understand. How is it we're linked when you've not yet claimed me?" Apparently, the bond fully formed once they exchanged bites. A primitive method but it didn't surprise him. The exchange of rings and other trinkets derived from human tradition.

She shrugged. "I don't know why you and I are already connected. Perhaps it's fate. I've heard of it happening with some mated couples, but not often. No one knows why it happens with some pairings and not others. I have something similar with my twin, although we can't talk as clearly. With others in my family Sept, I can sense strong emotions if I'm close enough, but with you...it's like we are joined."

"It's freaky." On the one hand, he enjoyed the connection between them. He felt what she did when she let her guard down. An incredible experience when she sucked him, but outside of sex...he couldn't hide. *And I have so much darkness I don't want her to see.*

"Afraid I'll know all your secrets?" she teased.

"You already do." Except for the one he kept trying to deny: *I think I'm in love with her.*

The very idea terrified him. He loved his family, and it had gotten used against him. He couldn't protect them. Hell, he couldn't even manage to save himself.

Loving Aimi scared the fuck out of him because it meant he had to do anything he could to keep her safe, even if it meant sacrificing himself.

That was why he locked down his thoughts, why he wouldn't let her in because, if she knew what he planned, she'd probably rip his dick off.

Her eyes drooped. Blinked. Her head bobbed. Her gaze narrowed. "Whha-t did you do to me?" she slurred.

"Protecting my treasure."

"Assh—" She slumped forward, and he

caught her before she face planted.

He rubbed his face in her hair and whispered, "I'm sorry. But I have to do this alone." He carried her to the bedroom and stretched her onto the bed.

She looked so peaceful in her sleep. But boy, would she be pissed when she woke. He planned to be far away when the drugs wore off, and she roused spitting mad. He only hoped she'd stay asleep until after he'd rescued his sister or, knowing her as he already did, she'd arrive, ready to eviscerate him.

The clothing she'd ordered arrived within minutes of him tucking her in. The bellhop, a young fellow who stuttered a thank you when Brand slipped him a twenty, laid two garment bags on the sofa. The hotel employee also delivered two boxes of shoes and a bag with a certain famous brand of undergarments on the outside. Nothing but the best for his moonbeam.

Everything fit to perfection, even the underwear. He couldn't help but dangle the scrap she'd ordered for herself, a lacy little thong that he crushed in his fist for a moment. How he would have loved to peel the panties from her.

Don't get distracted. He dropped the lacy item and finished getting ready. He'd no sooner dressed in the tuxedo—a first for him as he'd skipped high school prom thinking it lame—than the phone in the room rang to let him know that his ride had arrived.

Performing one last check to make sure he looked presentable, he grimaced in the mirror, not recognizing himself and not just because he wore his human face—albeit older and leaner than he recalled—but because he couldn't help but see himself differently: taller, straighter, more confident than he recalled.

He blamed Aimi. She'd taken a man broken and almost ready to give up and seen something in him, something that flourished in her presence.

It's called pride. No longer was he reacting and allowing someone to control him. Brandon was his own man—in a fucking tuxedo, replete with cummerbund and shoes. Aimi had certainly been busy while he showered. He planned to be busier while she napped.

Before he could leave, he checked on her one last time, retucking the covers around her and ensuring a pillow cradled her head. He even brushed a soft kiss on her lips. She didn't react. He felt nothing through their link, her drugged sleep rendering it inert.

"Goodbye, moonbeam." When next she woke, he'd be out of her life.

He didn't look back as he left. Couldn't or he might change his mind.

When he arrived in the lobby, the desk clerk pointed to the car out front that had arrived to drive him to the party. Except it wasn't a regular car. Nope, not for his moonbeam. She'd ordered a bloody limo with a driver and everything.

Sigh. He was so out of his element with her. Upon exiting the hotel, a driver—dressed in a black suit replete with hat—tipped his head and held open the passenger door at the back. He tried refusing. Apparently, that wasn't an option.

"Company policies, sir," the driver stated. "All clients are to sit in the back."

With no choice, the imposter in his new outfit sat in the backseat of a limo feeling utterly out of his element.

Nothing wrong with dressing nice. Nice involved clean jeans and a button-down shirt. This tuxedo thing constricted and choked.

The driver knew where to go apparently, and so Brand got to sit back and wait to be delivered to the devil. It gave him time to ponder his course of action. His current plan involved showing up at the front door and brazening his way in.

Who's got the biggest balls now, Uncle?

Brash pride shouldn't take the place of intelligence, though. Should he have opted for subterfuge? He could have. He had a location. Brandon could arrive in stealth, and possibly exit the same way.

Then again, why should he hide anymore? After everything his uncle had done, wasn't it Brandon's turn to be in the sunlight? No longer did Brandon have to conceal himself. He wasn't a monster—on the outside. Inside, he seethed with cold rage and a hunger for vengeance.

Crunch his bones. Grind him down.

Let his uncle try and play his games face-to-face with Brandon. He'd take care of him. However, Aimi and her family made good points when they claimed a public event such as this would have Uncle Theo on his best behavior. The public would be watching, and as usual in today's age of intrusive media, they would judge. If Brand showed himself, his uncle could do nothing to stop him, not without causing questions.

There is nothing stopping me from getting to see and talk to my sister. Should they choose to leave together, what could Uncle Theo do? Nothing without causing a scene.

Speaking of a scene, Brand just about screamed like a girl when, at a stoplight, the passenger door opened, and a silver-haired dervish sat down. The car lurched into motion as he gaped. Finally, he managed to say, "Aunt Waida?" Who else would wear a ball gown of bright fuchsia hung with tassels?

"It's me, in the flesh, boy. Don't look so surprised. You didn't seriously think we'd let you walk into the den of that wolf alone, did you?"

"Why wouldn't you? I'm not family."

Whack. The cuff barely rocked him, and Waida tsked. "You're with my niece. That makes you family by proxy."

"I'm not with her."

That earned him another cuff. "Idiot. Lucky for you, I've got something that might cure your affliction."

"What affliction?"

"The one making you stupid. I know what you did and have to say I have a new admiration for your balls, and not just because they're brave." She eyed him in a way that made him want to wear more layers of clothes. "You are a rather interesting fellow. A pity you won't live long. Drugging my niece." The aunt chuckled. "She'll make you pay for that."

"I did it to protect her."

"She won't see it that way."

He already expected Aimi to get mad. That didn't stop him from doing what he had to. "What are you doing here?"

"I left not long after meeting you. My psychic—"

"You take advice from a psychic?" The disdain might have dripped a little.

"Say it like that again and you'll see why I'm not the nice sister."

"You mean there's a nice one of you?" He wasn't being completely sarcastic.

"Ungrateful, and after all the work I went to. Who do you think made the arrangements for the limo and whatnot? Can't trust those who aren't family these days. Always doing things with ulterior motives."

"And what's your motive?"

"The glory of the family, of course. A little fun, maybe some mayhem, that's good, too. Although I'll deny it if Zahra asks."

The flippant answer irritated. "This isn't a game."

"Everything in life is a game. Best you learn that now. Especially since you're one of the pieces."

"Nice to know I have a use as a peon."

"Stop disparaging yourself. It's annoying. By now, even with your dense skull, you should realize that you are an important player, or are you going to continue denying the events that keep unfolding around you?"

"I didn't ask for any of this to happen. I was a victim of science. Nothing more. I'm not a dragon."

Whack. The slap to the side of his head didn't completely capture him by surprise, but bracing for it didn't completely account for the sting.

"What the fuck?"

"Language," snapped the matron aunt. "Where we are going, people will be listening, and they won't offer you any respect or support if you come across as a backwoods hillbilly whinebag with a woe-is-me complex."

"But I am a backwoods hillbilly." As to the rest…whining seemed better than giving in to the rage and rampaging.

Rampaging is more fun. Things sometimes get crunched.

"Manner is as manners does. Wealth has nothing to do with it. Do you really think everyone you will meet tonight came from blue blood? Most of them will be commoners. Beneath me. Beneath you. Throw your shoulders back, hold your chin high, and act as if you are the most important person in the room. Because, if my sister's tests are right, you are."

"And if I'm not?"

"Then fake it, but for bloody sakes, stop moaning about it."

"Or what?" Yes, he'd poked the dragon with a verbal stick on purpose.

Slitted eyes spitting green fire fixed him. "You don't want to know."

The limo stopped for another light, and just as quickly as she'd arrived, Waida slid from the car, only to have another silver-haired woman take her place.

Aimi, smelling delightful and looking even more delicious, took the seat across from him. He blamed the sight of her thigh peeking from her dress through the high slit for not tossing her out and telling the driver to hit the gas.

Alas, he was weak. So weak before her. He groaned. "What are you doing here? I left you safe at the hotel."

"You know there are laws against drugging

women."

"I did it to keep you safe."

"No, you did it because you're chivalrous."

Flinched. "Am not."

"Not completely, given you drugged me. Good thing I expected it."

"If you knew, then why eat the food?"

She rolled a bare shoulder—that needed one more thing to make it perfect. A bite mark. His to be more precise.

"I ate it because I was hungry. Also, I needed a nap and, given my aroused state, because someone didn't follow through"—glare—"I needed a little help."

"That doesn't explain how you got here. I left almost an hour ago."

"You did. The limo's been driving around the city streets close to the hotel. Long enough for me to catch a power nap and get ready."

"You mean you planned this all along?"

"With a little help. Aunt Waida wanted to see if anyone would jump the car if it were just you in it. She was most disappointed when nothing happened."

"Maybe they've given up."

"Doubtful. It's more likely they knew of the surveillance and are planning an ambush later on."

"How is it your aunt is here on the advice of a psychic, but no one else is?"

"My mother never puts all her resources into one location. In this case, though, I'll wager Waida acted as an independent. She is a matriarch in her own right, even if her Sept consists only of her husband and her one son."

"But how did she get here? From the sounds of it, she got here before us, but we were on the only flight."

"As if she'd trust a commercial airline. She flew herself."

"She flew as a dragon?" He made sure to hush the words in case the driver listened. The partition separated him from the front, but his paranoia was on full alert. "Isn't that like sacrosanct?"

"She flew as in a twin-engine turboprop. She dislikes traveling any distance by car and says if she can't use her own wings then she'll control the ones she does use."

"Your family is very determined."

"As are you. We will make gloriously stubborn children."

He sighed. "You don't give up, do you?"

"Nope. Neither should you because I am the ultimate prize."

More like an impossible dream, but he clamped that thought down tightly, lest she slap him.

The limo headed toward their destination, or so he assumed, and he didn't know what to think. Having Aimi by his side proved distracting, but even worse, he couldn't hide the fact that he headed into enemy territory. More than ever he questioned the wisdom of waltzing in.

The lights of the city were left behind as they drove into suburbia. Wide streets, towering trees, actual sidewalks, and lawns lit with strategic emphasis to showcase trees and shrubbery, manicured to within an inch of its verdant green life.

They slowed down at a gate, the wide archway spanning the lanes entering and exiting. There was a very ornate welcoming sign and even a guardhouse where someone with a tablet briefly spoke to the driver before letting them enter. It appeared they entered a gated community for the wealthy, a place where the rich went to live and remain separated from the masses.

This was where Parker lived? It seemed too lavish even for his uncle. "Are we going to the right place?" he asked.

"It's what the invitation said."

The location might be right. However, it seemed wrong because, when Brand thought of a birthday party, what came to mind were the celebrations of his youth. The backyard decked in Christmas lights strung among the trees, the multi-colored bulbs seeming suspended in midair once darkness fell. The several picnic tables—the wood spongy with age and mildewed by time—covered by plastic covers with balloons and *Happy Birthday* emblazoned upon it. For added decoration, a few colored balloons on strings taped to the house and branches. The simple décor went well with the menu of barbecued burgers, hot dogs, and macaroni salad followed by dessert; a slab cake his ma made from scratch, smeared in icing with candles of varying heights staggered all over it. In their house, even little things like candle stubs were reused to save money.

The tight budget also meant it was only close family and the very best of friends invited because, as his mother often said, "We aren't feeding the whole damned neighborhood." It might have sounded harsh and uncaring, but that was the reality of living on a budget. Despite the restrictions, no Mercer ever felt forgotten, even if some of the presents arrived still in a plastic bag, with tags, and possibly five-fingered instead of bought.

But it was the thought that counted.

So was it any wonder when he heard the celebration was for his sister's birthday that Brand kind of expected something intimate and familiar? The hoity-toity houses in the area with their tall gates and stone-walled fences said otherwise.

I should have guessed by the tuxedo and limo. The suit Aimi had made him wear was anything but simple, but he assumed she'd ordered them because that was what rich girls did.

He tugged at the collar of the button-down shirt. "Damned thing is choking me."

"Don't play with it. It's perfect."

No, she was perfect in the shimmering gown of mauve, threaded with silver. Aimi's hair fell in a silky curtain and tickled the top of her ass.

My ass. Funny how he'd fallen into her habit of thinking of her as his.

How on earth was he going to walk away from her when this surely failed mission was done?

"Why the grim face? Tonight we get your sister back."

"Or everything goes to hell."

"If Parker touches a hair on my head, my mother will have his balls for breakfast, with a dash of salt and covered in a Béarnaise sauce."

"That's if there's anything left after I'm done with him." The very idea of Aimi getting hurt chilled the blood in his veins, but it didn't bother him. More and more he noticed the line between him and his other self fading. *What am I saying? I don't even think there's a separation anymore.* His thoughts, emotions, everything seemed to come from him, with a new twist.

"You'd kill someone for me?" she asked.

"In a heartbeat."

"You say the sweetest things."

Ignoring the passing mansions, he turned to her. "Can I ask you something? If I'm not a gold dragon, hell, if it turns out you're wrong and I'm not dragon at all, would you still want me?"

"You forget, I claimed you even before we knew you might be gold."

"Because you thought I was a dragon. What if I'm not?"

She leaned forward, the scent of her an intoxicating perfume that wrapped around his senses. "My mother might disown me, but I don't really care what you are. Gator, dragon, or just a man. I think it's past time we paired with who we're meant to be with and not just because our genes are a perfect match."

"You think we're a perfect match?" The very idea stretched credulity.

"Don't you?"

He wanted to say, "No, hell no," but he couldn't because, damn it all, he wanted to be her perfect mate. Wanted her grace to temper his rough edges, wanted his strength to be her shield, wanted her soft words to soothe the beast inside.

Come here.

He didn't say the words aloud, but she heard him and didn't move. "Not now. Later."

"Fuck that." Who knew if there would be a later? He reached over and pulled her onto his lap.

A shocked gasp parted her lips, and she only

put up a small fight. "Brand, we shouldn't, my makeup."

He didn't care about her makeup. She looked just as good, and he personally thought better, without it. Besides, he wanted to taste those perfect pink lips. "It's not cherry flavored," he murmured as he slanted his mouth over hers, noting the bland taste.

"I'll make sure to buy some for you then for next time."

Because there would be a next time. Many of them. He grabbed her hair in his fist, luxuriating in the silken feel of it. She moaned against his mouth, and she opened the link between them enough that he could feel her excitement at his slightly rough handling of her. His moonbeam might appear prim and dainty on the outside, but inside, she was a wild thing who liked to get dirty.

With me. And only me.

The slit in the skirt of her dress meant his hand could move to caress the flesh of her thigh then upward until he encountered the lacy barrier of her panties.

Rip.

"Brand!"

"You don't need these."

"I can't go in public not wearing underpants. It's not done." She huffed it, and yet he could sense the thread of excitement at the thought.

"I don't want anything in my way when I take you later." Because he was going to take a page out of her book and assume they would prevail. His luck was changing. He was no longer a victim. The time had come for him to be the hero.

And heroes always got the girl.

A shiver went through her. "You are a tease."

"Why, because I like to do this?" He fingered her, feeling the honey on his finger and wishing it were his tongue.

"Because I know we don't have time to do this right now."

"You're right. We don't." But he wanted to. He withdrew his hand and licked the finger. As if he'd let that ambrosia go to waste.

She growled. "I swear, if you keep teasing, I might just claim you in front of everyone and to hell with the media." Her violet eyes slitted and flashed with fire, a sign he'd come to recognize that meant strong emotions rode her.

"I'm almost to the point I might just let you do that, moonbeam." Because she wasn't the only one tired of this game they played.

"Do you like me, Brand?" she asked with the most serious mien.

"More than I should, moonbeam."

The limo slowed as they turned, and Aimi slid off his lap, grumbling about needing to "Fix my lipstick and hair." But the bond connecting them let him know the grumbling was just a façade; inside, she practically burst with happiness.

I did that. He'd made her happy. Brandon wasn't sure if he'd ever done that before for someone other than his mother, but he knew he sure as heck liked it. After he saved his sister, maybe he should rethink his decision to leave.

He peeked out the window as Aimi pouted her lips to reapply her gloss. They were passing a long, fenced stretch of land, each of the houses in this area occupying large plots of property. Anxiety gripped him. He tugged at the damned choking collar. "My sister won't recognize me in this monkey suit."

"Stop complaining. We can't just show up in street clothes. They'll never even let us past the gate."

"Gates and guards and fences. What is this, Fort Knox?"

"More like the wolf's den."

And she meant that quite literally. It had taken some digging, but according to Aimi, her sister Adi had discovered that Parker owned the property they were going to tonight. Hidden beneath layers of shell companies, they'd found three locations directly linked to Parker. Tonight, they would visit the West Coast mansion, but his uncle also owned two other properties. One a simple townhouse on the East Coast in New York itself, and the other, down in Texas, was a several-hundred-hectare estate that not only boasted a house that could have fit a decent chunk of the Mercer family but also a series of outbuildings because the property doubled as a ranch.

"My Uncle Parker is a farmer?" That didn't seem right.

"On paper he is. Although, he doesn't seem to sell much cattle. This is his entertaining house we are going to tonight. The one he's been using to kiss up to government officials."

"And you're sure Sue-Ellen is going to be there?"

"Where else would the birthday girl be for her party?"

It occurred to him in that moment that, while

he'd done lots of bitching and moaning—in a manly fashion, of course—about everything that'd happened, he'd yet to do one really important thing. "Thank you."

"For what?"

"For doing all this. For finding out where my sister is."

"I can't take all the credit. My sister helped a little." At his arched brow, she laughed. "Okay, a lot. But you shouldn't thank me for that. What your uncle did to your sister is wrong, and now we're going to make it right."

"I don't know what I did to deserve this, but thank you."

"Don't thank me." She leaned forward and touched his knee, and said softly, "From here on out, even if you don't believe it yet, we are one. What affects you, affects me. Those you care about are also now under my charge, my protection."

That kind of partnership, the very idea of it, damn near took his breath away. Looking at her, her platinum perfection with her slender elegance contrasted with his darker appearance, and even darker, colder blood. Over and over he kept seeing reasons why she deserved better than him. A mere lowly Mercer thinking he could be with this gorgeous beauty? Except she looked just right by his side, her silvery hair a complement to his dark, her slim and graceful beauty emphasizing his bulk.

And he was going to bring her into possible danger?

Not for the first time, he tried to talk her out of it. "I don't think—" She wasn't interested in his arguments, so she muffled his protest with a kiss.

Which made him wonder if he'd protested on purpose.

Duh. Him or his other half talking? He couldn't tell anymore.

The limo pulled to a stop, and he peered out at the crazy-big mansion with its stone columns and massive banks of windows. Lights streamed from all of them, and he could almost hear his mother yell, "Turn off the damned lights. You're just burning money."

The driver opened the door for them and stood to the side. It was then that Brandon noticed that, while the face wasn't familiar, edges of silver hair peeked from the cap. More reinforcements.

He slid out of the car and then held out his hand as he'd seen the actors do when they tread the red carpet—and he and his buddies mocked them over a few beers. They only watched it to see the hot actresses in their revealing dresses.

Aimi stepped out, a ray of moonlight that stole all argument and breath from him.

"Ready?" she asked, linking her hand through his arm and resting it on his bicep.

"No."

The tinkle of her laughter washed over him, soothing some of his nerves. "Let us go fetch your sister, that we might make better use of that hotel room tonight."

"That confident, are you?"

"Losing is never an option."

That had never been truer than tonight. Still, though, he couldn't help but wonder what he'd gotten himself into, given that he felt completely out of his element. Sure, he wore the damned suit, with its choking tie, and looked the part, but he was convinced everyone around him could see he was swamp-born.

It's all about attitude, at least according to the dragon ladies. So he faked it. He held his head high, his shoulders back, put on a scowl for anyone who dared look at him—and a deadly promising glare for anyone who stared at his moonbeam.

Within, his cold half didn't say a word, maybe because it no longer had to. Was Aimi right? Had he and his beast somehow, in all the turmoil, become one entity?

Tonight wasn't the night to ponder it. He had to concentrate on his mission: saving Sue-Ellen and getting both her and Aimi back out, alive. He wouldn't make the same promise for his uncle. As far as he was concerned, the world would be a better place without Theo.

The good thing about attending a public event, as Aimi had explained before their first aborted flight, was the fact that Parker couldn't try anything overt. There would be people in attendance, humans and dignitaries, as well as some media. There would be cameras everywhere, the eyes of the world on them as Parker pretended for the masses that shifters were normal, that he was normal. If by *normal*, psychopaths counted.

As their limo pulled away, he glanced back and noted a line of cars, luxury ones along with more limos, crawled up the drive, disgorging passengers at the tiered front stoop.

He tugged at his collar again, noting all the guys wore suits while the ladies glittered and wowed with their rainbow-colored gowns and teetering heels.

"Remember, no punching your uncle," she admonished just before they reached the front door and the people checking the guests against lists on their handheld tablets.

But he deserves it. A thought pushed instead of spoken aloud where security could hear him and escort him out. Uncle Theo had earned more than a good fist to the face. Every breath the man took was a waste, and Brandon intended to be the one to put a stop to it.

The guy in the dark suit manning the entrance tapped his screen. "Welcome, Ms. Silvergrace. Might I inquire as to whom your guest is?"

Brandon expected many things but not her, "This is Brandon Mercer, Mr. Parker's missing nephew and the birthday girl's brother. But I do hope you'll keep it a surprise."

Highly unlikely, and he had to wonder why she'd announced it as they were waved into the house. He immediately pulled her aside to hiss, "Are you out of your fucking mind? Are you trying to fail this endeavor before we begin?"

"On the contrary, we've just made it harder for Parker to screw with us. We've just publicly announced who we are, thus making it harder for you to just disappear, or hadn't you noticed the people behind us eavesdropping?"

A glance behind showed him a couple whispering excitedly.

"So everyone knows we're here. Great. We've just given my uncle warning that he needs to hide my sister again."

"Have some faith, dear fiancé. Your uncle is

much too full of himself to let something like your reappearance make him do something the media might notice, such as hide the birthday girl."

"I hope you're right," he muttered as she led him farther into the mansion. Not so long ago, he might have been more impressed by the polished tile floors and the detailed plaster moldings. However, he'd spent a bit of time in the Silvergrace abode, and had to say he thought their taste much classier and definitely less gaudy.

Disdain curled Aimi's lip. "Good grief, did he seriously mix nineteenth-century Impressionism with postmodern art?" Aimi uttered a noise of polite disgust. "Wannabe."

"They both look shitty to me. I don't see why anyone would pay money for any of them." He swept a hand to encompass the wall of art with its scribbled and abstract offerings.

"Mixing is one thing. However, that doesn't mean the art itself is bad. Don't you see the talent? Look closer. Look again with the eyes of one who covets treasure," she added.

What did she mean? It all looked like paint smears to him, except he noticed, when he did pay more attention, that the brush strokes on the paintings that at first had seemed choppy and uneven actually portrayed a snapshot scene; whereas the other style, using the same kind of bold strokes, was of nothing.

But, even noting those differences, he could easily say, "Still don't see the appeal of either."

"I'll have to show you the stuff I've got hidden in my hoard. I promise you'll see the value."

Was Aimi showing off her treasures the

equivalent of giving him a key? Where was a meddling Silvergrace when he had a question?

Step by step, he flowed deeper into the place and the further he went, the more the back of his neck prickled. Danger. But where?

Looking around, he noted everyone in their tuxedos and lavish gowns. Some paid attention to him and Aimi, mostly Aimi, but that seemed normal given her extreme beauty. More glances showed a lot of security—a faint sniff revealed them as shifter security, along with some males who didn't smell at all. Not human or shifter. It reminded him of the plane.

"Are those more of those wyvern dudes?" he murmured to her under the guise of drawing her close to let a server with drinks pass by.

"Yes, they are, and they are making no attempt to hide their presence. Mother won't like that."

"Why? Does this mean Parker was working with the ones that attacked the plane and then our car?"

"Possibly. Although I find it hard to believe any of the Septs would align with him. But then again, your uncle has done many things of late considered impossible."

"Speaking of my uncle, there he is." Standing across the room from them, looking as polished as ever for a mangy wolf, stood his uncle, Theo. He wore a black tuxedo like everyone else but had paired it with a light blue shirt that matched the blue of his wife's gown. Brandon clenched his fists at his side, wanting so badly to wipe that smug smile off the bastard's face, but he couldn't. He had to behave because of who stood by Parker's side, his sister Sue-Ellen dressed in a buttercup-yellow gown. For a moment, he just stared. How could he not? His sister shone, her smile bright as she shook hands with well-wishers, pasting on a fake smile for the masses.

Not for much longer. Time to end her nightmare.

"That's my sister. I am going to talk to her."

"Wait until I distract your uncle and then snag her."

He probably didn't want to know but… "How are you going to distract him?"

"You'll see." Aimi gave him a smile that might have bordered on feral. It served only to make her more beautiful—*but don't forget she is deadly.*

Off she swished, her slender hips undulating and causing the violet sheen of her gown to shimmer. She snared a fluted glass of wine, and he heard her exclaim, "You call this swill champagne? I don't even feed this to my staff at Christmas."

The fine art of snobbery in action. As Aimi caused a titter and commotion with her entitled rich-girl airs, Brandon made his way around the outer edge of the room, watching his uncle and sister. When Parker aimed himself in Aimi's direction, Brandon made his move, sidling through the remaining crowd until he stood behind his sister, the scent of her true essence masked with some kind of flowery fragrance.

He spun her around and grabbed her in a hug. "I'm so glad to see you."

"Release me at once," she screeched. "Security."

"Sue-Ellen, it's me," he exclaimed, putting her down. "The real me. I'm not a monster anymore."

And, no, he didn't care who heard him. Because of Parker, everyone knew Brandon was a shifter. They just didn't know about the extras done to him.

His excitement at finding his sister didn't seem returned, given Sue-Ellen's glare.

"What are you doing here?"

"Rescuing you, at last."

Her brow creased. "Rescuing me from what? I don't need anyone to save me, and you'll ruin everything if you don't leave."

"Leave? Are you on drugs? I've been trying to get to you for months, ever since the Bittech blowup. I'm sorry it took so long, but Parker's been hard to track down. But now that I'm here, you can leave. He won't dare stop us with all these people watching." In that, he hoped Aimi was right. He grabbed his sister's hand and would have pulled her, but she yanked free.

"What are you doing?" his sister asked.

"Leaving and you're coming with me."

"Why?"

"Because Uncle Theo is a kidnapping psycho. But you don't have to worry anymore. Once we get out of here, I'll make sure he never finds you again." He didn't quite know yet how he'd manage it, but surely his mother and brothers could help him hide her.

"There seems to be a misunderstanding. I don't want to leave."

He blinked as he digested her words. "I don't understand."

"What's there not to understand? I don't want to go with you."

"But why? Surely you can't want to stay?

Uncle Theo is evil."

"According to you. I happen to think differently."

"He's brainwashed you."

"Do you think I'm that stupid? Use your head for something other than a hat rack," his sister snapped. "Do you really think he could have kept me all this time if I didn't want to be kept? Do you really think me so helpless?"

"Then why didn't you escape?"

"Because I wanted to stay." Her chin tilted. "Uncle Theo took me from the bayou, from that pigsty we called a home. He bought me nice clothes. Made sure I got a proper education."

"He experimented on me and the others. Kept you hostage. He told the world our secret."

A sneer pulled his sister's lips. "A secret that was leaking all over the place anyhow, or are you so out of touch with the modern world that you never watched any of the *YouTube* videos? He just confirmed what many in the world already knew."

"And what about what he did to me? To the others?"

"He made some mistakes, but what he was doing, and still continues to do with the Bittech research, is for the greater good. He wants to make shifters great."

"He made me into a monster," he growled. "He took away my freedom and made me do things I would have never done."

"He took a chance and, as many have on the path to greatness, suffered setbacks."

Hearing his sister defend the man he'd hated for so long was worse than any bullet or slap. The fact that she justified the things done to Brandon hurt, but what hurt worse was the realization that he couldn't change Sue-Ellen's mind. She truly believed Theo had committed no crimes. His own sister didn't care what happened to him.

I'm such a fucking idiot. Worse than an idiot. He felt betrayed.

"I hope to God you remember this conversation when he turns on you one day," was his bitter reply as he spun away from his sister.

"Where are you going?" his sister asked. "I know he'll want to talk to you. He's been looking for you."

"Tell him to go to Hell."

He was done here. *I should have never come.* Time to find Aimi and go.

Chapter Sixteen

It didn't take the bond between them for Aimi to notice the conversation between Brand and his sister went poorly. Brand went from overjoyed at seeing her to shocked and then angry.

Time to save him before he did something he would regret. But at least he'd seen for himself what Adi had discovered.

"The girl's not a prisoner," her twin had stated during her phone call while he'd showered at the hotel.

"Not an obvious one, of course. Brand says the uncle is holding her hostage for good behavior. She's probably too terrified to leave."

"So terrified she's been out shopping all over Beverly Hills."

"That doesn't mean anything."

But the more Adi revealed—Sue-Ellen's car, a zippy red convertible that she liked to race according to speeding tickets, and the clubs she went partying at until the wee hours—it didn't surprise Aimi when Sue-Ellen pulled away from her brother and gave him her back.

Through their bond, she felt the betrayal, and she wanted to soothe him. She knew he'd have to learn about his sister's defection to Parker's side himself. He would have never believed it otherwise.

Mission accomplished. Time to leave, and fuck the possible gold egg or dragon Parker might have. Right now, Brand was more important. Let the others scout out the possible gold. She already had hers.

She weaved through the crowd, looking to make her way to his side, only to find her arm caught in an iron grasp.

She turned her head to see a man with silver temples held her. "If it isn't Uncle Theo."

"And you must be Zahra's daughter, Aimi. I was told you were attending, and with my nephew. Such a pleasure to meet you, especially since you found the missing boy."

"No thanks to you. I know what you did."

"What I did? You make it sound like I did something wrong, and yet, all I've ever done is try to better my family's lot in life, and what does my ungrateful nephew do? He turns against me and shacks up with a dragon."

"Shhh." His blatant words brought on a panic instilled by years of hiding. "What do you think you're doing?" Did he not know how the game was played in public?

"We are having a conversation. Would you prefer we conduct it somewhere more private?"

Yes. Because then she could do what she'd warned Brand not to; punch Parker in the face. She allowed Parker to lead her away from the busy ballroom area down a hall into a quiet section of the house. The room they entered had to be his office, or so the giant desk seemed to indicate.

Out of the sight of curious eyes, she

wrenched free from Parker and put a few feet between them. "I don't know what you think you are doing, but it is going to stop. We know you are holding a gold prisoner."

"Not just a gold," Parker advised with a smirk.

"You've got more dragons?" The very idea flustered her. What to reply; especially since he didn't seem the least bit repentant or worried about telling her?

"I've got many things in my labs." Said with a hint of smugness.

"Release them at once. We won't stand for you playing games with our kind."

"Demands? You're not in a position to make demands of me, little girl. I hold all the cards. You seem to forget that I know your secret."

"A secret you'd better not divulge. Or else." She narrowed her eyes in clear threat.

"Or else what? You seem to think you can threaten me, and yet, I find myself very ambivalent about it. One of the things I've learned is, while many threaten, few have the balls to follow through. You can say whatever you like. I really don't care." Parker trailed his fingers over the desktop as he circled it. He dropped into the leather chair behind it and tucked his hands over his belly.

If her mother had taught her one thing growing up, it was to never concede that someone had influence over you. The moment a person did that, they lost their bargaining power. "You should care, because once I tell Mother you're holding our kind prisoner, chances are there won't be any remains left." Actually, Aimi should change shapes right now and incinerate him herself. Two problems with that scenario; one: possible discovery by roaming guests or staff, not to mention recording devices. And second, she wasn't sure if her gift had regenerated enough to work.

"There will be no retaliation or attacks on me or any of my establishments because if you do, then your secret comes out."

"Are you threatening me?"

"You. Your family. All the dragon Septs, actually. Anyone who isn't human should heed me. The rights I am fighting for will benefit us all. Therefore, it's only fair you support the cause, willingly or not."

"You made the choice to out the shifters."

"Dragons are shifters, too."

"We want no part in your rebellion." The right thing to say but a small part of her couldn't help but admire the Cryptozoids' ability to escape the shadows. *I covet their freedom.* Even if it came with a price in blood. It should be noted there were few moments in history where major change happened that didn't involve a little war and mayhem.

Was Parker's vision truly that bad? For the first time since their ignoble defeat, the dragons could think of reentering the world scene, and all because Parker had paved the way.

But her opinion was hers alone. The Septs should be the one to make the choice, not Aimi, and most definitely not Parker.

A sneer twisted his lips. "You think your kind is so high and mighty with your power and money. But you're cowards. A dying breed. Undeserving of what you have. Just because you don't know how to make full use of your might doesn't mean others can't. You've seen what I can do."

"You mean what science can do."

At this, his expression turned sly. "You're speaking of my nephew. I am sure my scientists will be quite interested in learning how Brandon managed to change his shape. He's the first, you know. A shining example some would say of the Mercers' solid genes."

"You experimented on him. Your own family. Spliced him with a dragon."

"And if I did? Science must sometimes sacrifice a few for the greater good. But in this case, shouldn't you thank me? I hear you came to the party together. A dragoness about to hit her prime and a male, unclaimed. Have you not seen the possibilities yet? I am aware of how few males you spawn each generation. It's a struggle to maintain the family lines, and I know you've had to rely on science these past few decades to ensure you don't completely die out. What if a fresh stash of males suddenly came onto the scene?"

Artificial insemination and fertility treatments were a boon to the dragons. But it had also introduced the twenty-eight rule. "Are you trying to tell me you're going to sell male dragons to us?"

"If the price is right, but I think more profit can be made simply by using the males my labs create as breeding stock."

"We are not cattle."

"And yet your own rules have turned you into brood mares. How long before you carry some random fetus, a baby or two to continue your line?" Because even the women who couldn't find a mate needed to produce an heir. It was the rule of the Septs.

"I have a mate."

"For now. Did Brandon tell you what happened to the other patients who received the same DNA splice?" The wide smile much resembled that of the wolf before he ate the little girl in the red cape. "The others all went a little loco. It wasn't pretty. So many bodies to hide."

"You're sick. You sit here bragging about your exploits, are proud you experimented on people against their will. Your own family even. It's wrong. You can't use Cryptozoids as test subjects, and you most certainly won't get away with keeping dragons captive for your experiments."

"But I already have." His brow arched. "And I'm not done collecting them yet. It's like a game of *Pokémon Go*. Can I collect them all? How many color Septs are there? There's silver like you, then the reds, of which there are many shades, the blues, and greens. Mustn't forget the blacks and the whites with the shades of gray, too. Oh, and gold."

"So you do admit you have a gold dragon."

"I never denied it. Would you like to meet him?"

The jaws of the trap loomed all around her, and Aimi realized just how badly she'd miscalculated. For some reason, she'd expected Parker to abide by a set of rules, civilized guidelines, but there was nothing civilized about the creature in front of her. He was evil, through and through. His ends did not justify the means.

He has to die.

She flung herself at him, knowing she couldn't

fully transform but having strength enough to pull forth the opal claws with their razor-sharp tips.

Parker proved fast, much faster than expected. The gun rose from where he'd kept it hidden under his desk, and he shot her at point-blank range.

She had only time for a mental yell, "It's a trap. Run!" before everything went dark.

Chapter Seventeen

The shout hit his mind with the force of a bomb, and Brandon shot out a hand, catching himself on a wall to keep himself from falling.

Aimi. The warning came from his moonbeam. What had happened? Where was she? He felt for the tendril connecting him to her, only to find it gone.

Gone?

Impossible. She couldn't be gone. He wouldn't allow her to die. Except he didn't think she was dead, more likely just asleep. Deeply asleep, and he knew who to blame.

Parker.

Fucking Parker. Playing games again, and this time with his moonbeam.

Like fuck.

I'm coming to get you, moonbeam, and woe to any dumb bastards who got in his way. He located the nearest guard and grabbed him by the lapels, yanking him off his feet and growling, "Where is my uncle?"

"Sir, you need to set me down and calm yourself."

"I'm going to twist your head off if you don't tell me where he is right now."

The guard chose instead to speak into his microphone. "We have a code expel on the main mezzanine." Of more importance than the warning, the guy completely ignored Brand's threat.

"You're going to be drinking out of a straw if you don't tell me where my uncle is."

"Sir, I'm going to ask once again that you set me down and exit the premises.

"Like fuck." As more than a few sets of eyes turned his way, he dropped the guard and swept the guy's ankles with a foot, tumbling him to the floor and giving him a boot for good measure. At the gaping mouths of a few nearby guests, he shrugged. "He grabbed my girlfriend's ass without her permission."

That seemed to satisfy a few, but he didn't linger. Already, Brandon could see more guards converging on his spot, so he headed deeper into the house. If Parker had nabbed Aimi, then he wouldn't have done so in public.

He has to have an office or something in this fucking place.

But where?

How about using my nose for something other than sniffing for fresh cookies?

Away from the main crush of people at the bash—and a sister who disappointed him on so many levels—he found it easier to sift the scents marking the air. So many aromas, but none of them belonged to Aimi. She truly was unique, which made him wonder how his kind had gone for so long not recognizing that dragons lived among them. Surely he wasn't the first to scent their distinctive flavor?

Can you really see Aimi and her family in the bayou? Not really, and the very fact of their existence served as a reminder that there was much in the world he didn't know. Much he didn't believe until the truth had grabbed him with her dragon claws.

Does this mean other creatures of legend exist, too? It boggled the mind to contemplate.

More wandering meant encountering a few guards, who, shortly after, met the floor up close and personal. He assumed an alarm had gone out, but he didn't care. Only one thing mattered. Finding Aimi.

Her scent hit him at a crossroads in the halls. With a clear trail to follow, he broke into a run. The guard that stepped into his way received an arm to the throat that heaved him into the air. The guy hit the floor hard and got trampled. The second idiot who thought to block his way lifted a gun.

"I wouldn't if I were you," Brandon snarled, his cold rage holding on by the barest thread. He couldn't completely stem the rage, though. His teeth elongated and flashed as his eyes narrowed. All of a sudden, he found himself very hungry.

Let's crunch some bones.

To his credit, the guard didn't budge, even though Brand changed. He even managed to fire off a shot, which Brand missed by ducking low. He dove forward to tackle the shooter around the knees.

Oomph. The guard hit the floor with Brand on top.

A quick twist and a crack was all it took before he was off again, only to find himself momentarily stymied by the thick portal in his way, the handle locked.

More of him morphed, muscles bulging and popping, a man not becoming a monster but rather using all the skills he had. He wrenched at the handle again and snapped it. The door still didn't quite give, but the remaining latch couldn't withstand the hard boot he gave it.

The door flung open, hitting the inside wall with a bang, but he was already through, landing in an office with a huge desk.

Aimi's scent hung in this space, and ended there, too.

The man behind all of Brandon's agitation stood behind his desk, hands tucked behind his back, that familiar smirk on his lips.

"Nephew, how nice of you to make an appearance."

Nice will be you spilling your blood on that expensive rug.

"Where is she?" Brand didn't hesitate to throw himself over the desk and grab his uncle by the lapels, slamming him into a wall.

It didn't shake Parker's cool confidence one iota. "No hello? You might be wearing a civilized outfit, but I see your manners are still lacking."

"Stop fucking blabbing and tell me where Aimi is."

"Of what concern is it of yours?"

"She's mine." Brand knew it was the wrong thing to growl as soon as it passed his hardening lips, but he couldn't stop himself.

"How fascinating. So you've claimed her."

He should have, but like an idiot, he'd let other things distract him from the most important thing.

"Tell me where she is." A request punctuated with slams of his uncle against the wall.

"She wanted to see a guest of mine, so I acceded to her wishes."

"If you've harmed her..." he warned in a low rumble, the cold in him seething with rage.

"Harm her? On the contrary, I have plans for her. She's a healthy female in her prime for breeding, and I have studs who will very much enjoy impregnating her."

Slam. Slam. Slam. The rough handling didn't stop his uncle's laughter.

"You can't do thisss," he huffed, feeling his control slip.

"I can, and will. And you can't stop me. But you can help. Since you seem attached to the girl, how about I give you first crack at poking her? Maybe you'll get lucky and plant your seed in her belly with your first attempt."

At that, he couldn't contain his rage anymore. He tossed his uncle, sending him flying across the room.

And still, the bastard laughed.

Brandon stalked toward Parker, seething and uncaring of the ripping fabric as the rest of him burst into view. He kept only his pants, kicking off the confining shoes. The shirt shredded, and yet the tie remained.

"So you can change back and forth at will." His uncle stood and wiped the blood from his lip. "Excellent. Most excellent. Perhaps your minor excursion won't be for naught. Now be a good boy and put this on."

From a pocket, his uncle pulled forth a collar. Not just any collar. Brandon's collar.

"I'm not putting that back on."

"Oh, you will, or Sue-Ellen—"

"Sue-Ellen made her choice. I am not

enslaving myself again to you for her."

"If not her, then how about your woman? Even now, your sedated paramour is being put on a copter for transport to my new facility. I think of it as Bittech four point oh."

For a moment, Brandon wondered what had happened to number three. But then the threat truly penetrated.

Did his uncle seriously think to hold Aimi against him? Brandon knew what would happen if he put that collar back on again. He also knew what his uncle would do to Aimi if he didn't.

He dropped to his knees and bowed his head, a beast before the madman who'd made him.

The collar dangled in front of him. "Put it on."

He intended to. Snatching the collar from his uncle's hands, Brandon shot to his feet and snapped it around Theo's neck before grabbing him by the hair and slamming his face into the wall a few times. Then cracked his neck for good measure before dropping the body.

Now we eat the flesh of the enemy.

Or maybe not.

In the distance, he could hear rotor blades, the sound of a helicopter warming up, which meant Aimi wasn't gone yet.

I'm coming, moonbeam. He wouldn't fail her. He couldn't and live with himself.

He slammed through the French doors, spilling into a courtyard illuminated only faintly by the lights shining from the windows in the house. Overhead, he could hear the whirring of the helicopter but could spot no access to the roof.

That's what wings are for, numbnut.

The chastisement launched him into the air, wings flapping, surely an incongruous sight with his shirt shredded and yet, somehow, his bowtie remaining. A classy-looking monster.

No, not a monster. A hybrid. Everyone kept telling him this shape was something special; it was time he believed it.

Wings working hard, he ascended until he found himself level with the rooftop. The chopper, a luxury thing with tinted windows, rose from its pad. He arrowed toward it, determined to get to it before it got too far.

The guards on the rooftop turned with their guns, a few even raised them, but none of them shot. An order was barked, "It's the nephew. Take him alive."

How did they plan to do that when they couldn't even reach him? Morons.

He angled toward the rising chopper, only to find his attention diverted.

What the fuck.

The fuck was a small dragon or, as Aimi called it with a sneer, a wyvern. It rose from the rooftop, and it wasn't alone. Just his luck. The damned guards weren't human.

Not good. Brandon prided himself on being a tough fucker. However, even he had limits, and he'd say a half-dozen flying pests might be it.

Giving up? Not an option, though, not with Aimi being held prisoner on that helicopter. He wasn't about to let her be taken away from him. No way would he allow anyone to torture her.

He needed to even the odds. But how? He

didn't have a gun. No weapon at all other than himself. His puny claws would prove no match against a half-dozen attacking at once.

Then change shape.

I did.

Not this shape. The other one.

My human shape? The one that didn't get along with gravity? How would that help?

Don't be dense. A chastisement that came from…himself?

It's time to stop denying what I am. Who I am.

And what was he?

Dragon.

He just had to accept it.

Sounded easy in theory but how did that work? The same way it always worked, by becoming.

For a moment, he hung in the air, wings spread wide, a dark, leathery angel in the sky with his eyes closed, waiting for a divine miracle.

If there truly is a dragon inside me, then I need you. Unlike the change to hybrid, and even when he used to be gator, the switch to dragon didn't hurt at all. Rather, it filled him with euphoria.

This is who I am!

He uttered a roar as he exploded, his body elongating, his tail a serpentine thrashing weapon, his wings bigger and mightier than ever.

His splendor stunned those preparing to attack. He hovered over them, a massive beast, filled with immense power and a burning in his lungs.

Breathe in. The words whispered to him, and he trusted his instinct. He sucked in deep.

Now blow out. It was almost as if a voice spoke to him, guided him in his new form, so he listened, expelling his breath and watching as a mist, green in hue with sparkling motes of gold, blasted forth and hit the approaching wyverns.

They tried to evade the mist; banking sharply for one, another rising rapidly while the others dropped. It didn't help them escape because it took only a touch, a simple speck, which sizzled on contact. Or so he assumed, given his attackers screamed and then changed, their wyvern shapes pulling back into their bodies until only the human was left. Humans with no wings that fell as gravity claimed them.

Splat.

That had to hurt, but he cared little for their plight, not when the metal cage holding his female kept moving.

How dare it defy me.

A mighty flap of his wings and he chased after it, his speed increasing as he felt the wakening of the thread between him and Aimi.

Whatever had masked it had now worn off, and he trilled, a trumpeting sound that echoed through the air.

Brand?

Her query hit him, and he could have laughed. Wait until she saw him.

He grabbed hold of the runners of the copter and pried open the door with the ease of a man peeling a banana. Someone immediately aimed a gun at his face for all of two seconds before Aimi shoved him out the opening. The scream halted abruptly once the body hit the ground.

The loveliest visage peered at him. "Holy shit, my mother is going to have fucking kittens. You ascended."

Fucking right, I did.

"And you're two-toned. Gold and green, but not the regular green of the emerald Sept. They will probably have kittens, too."

I am me.

"Yes, you are, and a fine-looking dragon, too. Very fine. My cousins will be so jealous."

You talk a lot.

"Sorry, you were here to rescue me, weren't you? Then let's make it good for the cameras."

With a smile on her lips, his moonbeam goddess leaped from the helicopter, and Brandon had to throw himself backwards to catch her.

And that was the picture that made it into the newspapers the following day.

Chapter Eighteen

"Of all the irresponsible things!" Aimi's mother still ranted. And guess what? It changed nothing.

"Untwist your panties. It was bound to happen. At least our exposure didn't occur because Aunt Joella got hungry and ate some villagers again."

"I think I would have preferred it." Her mother glowered at the newspaper article on her desk and its headline.

A dragon comes out of hiding to save a princess.

The accompanying image showed Brand, in his dragon glory, cradling Aimi in his claws.

The news sources, of course, went wild. It seemed more than a few photographers on the ground had caught part of the action in the sky, and the chopper covering the event overhead got excellent video footage of the whole thing.

Including Brand's superpower. *He can change people back to their true form.* Which begged the question, could it work in reverse? Aimi could already predict the problems that would ensue as science and governments tried to get their greedy hands on him.

Not on my watch. Brand belonged to her, and she'd do anything to keep him safe. Just like he did his utmost to try and protect her. He'd come to her rescue like a shining knight of old. Little did he know, Aimi didn't require rescue. But she couldn't deny it was cute when he did it.

The object of discussion currently drummed his fingers on the armrest of the chair in their hotel room. A hotel room a tad crowded, given Aunt Waida was there, as were all of Aimi's missing cousins and her sister. As for Mother Dearest, she was being projected live on the laptop, which meant it was easy to shut the lid and end her rant.

It didn't stop the chatter, the most notable part being that Parker wasn't dead as Brandon had hoped.

"Are you sure you wrung his neck? I've never heard of anyone who survived that before?" said cousin Babette.

"It's difficult but not impossible," countered Aunt Waida. "But I will add it takes a strong healing gene to get up and walk away."

Not just walk away but give a bloody news conference as the first tweets about the dragons in the sky began making their rounds.

"Dear people of the world, I tried to keep their secret, given their wishes to remain anonymous, but as you can see, that is no longer possible. You thought shifters were the only thing hiding among you. Wrong. And dragons are only the tip of the iceberg, and I cannot in good faith keep their secret anymore."

Thus did Parker toss all the Cryptozoids into the public eye from the mermaids deep in the oceans to the Sasquatch in the Rockies, from the djinn—who weren't at all what people thought—to the Yeti, who were already almost extinct. Even the last unicorn wasn't safe, as apparently, Parker had it captive on a wildlife preserve. To "keep it safe," or so he claimed with a smarmy grin.

Or maybe it wasn't captive. Perhaps, like Brand's sister, it, too, celebrated not having to hide anymore.

Aimi couldn't help but wonder if Parker had planned things this way, forced the dragons to out themselves. But surely he couldn't have predicted the evening's events? *Unless he has his own psychic.*

Despite all that had happened, Aimi couldn't deny that a certain part of her was relieved to not have to truly hide anymore, even if she cringed as her cousin Deka asked, "Do you think dragons will be the next *Twilight* romance?"

"She'd better make us sparkle if she does. I like bling."

"Maybe we'll get our own reality show. The Dragonesses of Dragon Point." Dragon Point not being so much a set place as where the Septs gathered to decide major issues.

"Out." Brand said the word quietly the first time, but when no one listened, he shouted it—in their heads.

OUT!

That got him more than a few blinks.

"Did he just…"

Nods all around. "Oh."

"Come along, we should leave the gold to his mate. Your Grace." Aunt Waida proffered a very short bow to Brand, but that was more than Aimi had ever seen her offer anyone before ushering all of her family out of the hotel room, leaving them gloriously alone.

"Since when can you shout in everyone's mind?"

"Since this." He grimaced as he raked his hand through his hair, highlighting the thick gold streak down the middle.

"It's because you ascended."

"I look like a skunk."

"Yet you smell like mine." She nuzzled his cheek, and a low rumble came from him. "And don't you owe me some pleasure."

"I didn't get my sister back."

"Not my fault she didn't want to come. Are you trying to get out of your promise to me?"

"Never. You are mine, moonbeam. Never forget it." Without warning, he nipped her on the shoulder, the gown she still wore leaving a good portion of her upper body bare. He bit her hard enough to break skin and leave a mark.

"You marked me." She shoved off his lap and planted her hands on her hips.

"I claimed you," he corrected.

"But I was supposed to claim you."

He shrugged. "I'm old-fashioned, which means the man goes first."

"If you're old-fashioned, then you should have done it during sex."

"Are you complaining about my methods?"

"Yes."

He stood and loomed over her, big, menacing...and hers. "Get your ass into that bedroom and onto that bed."

"Or?"

He snared her around the waist, and in a few

strides, was tossing her onto the mattress. She laughed as she hit it and bounced. Only one bounce since he landed atop her, his hands gripping hers, their fingers lacing together as he yanked her arms over her head. The position stretched her, while, at the same time, left her helpless under him.

"What are you planning to do now?" she asked, her words brushing softly against his lips.

"I plan to worship the center of my world."

"Are you sure you want this?"

He pressed himself against her, his erection clearly evident. "I'd say that's a yes."

For some reason, it was her turn to have doubts. "You do realize that, even if you're only partially gold, you could have any woman you want. The Septs would kill to have you marry into their family."

"But I found the family I want. The only woman I want."

"Good. Because had you answered; otherwise, I would have maimed you."

He laughed. "You are so fucking incredible."

"I know. It's what makes me the best treasure."

"The only treasure I need." His lips caught hers and claimed them with a fierce possessiveness that ignited her blood.

So much had happened, and so much remained unknown. But right here, right now, she didn't care. His world might revolve around her, but guess what; her world now revolved around him.

He's mine.

His lips blazed a trail across her jaw and then down her neckline. She panted and arched as he teased the swell of her breasts.

He didn't release her hands to pull down her dress. The savage tore it, using his teeth and brute strength.

"You do realize that dress was one of a kind, custom-made?"

"It was in my way."

The pure maleness of his reply served only to heighten her arousal, as did the swirl of his tongue as he teased the peak of her breast. The flat edges of his teeth nipped her nipple, and she cried out then cried again as he sucked her breast into his mouth. How she enjoyed the way he pulled on her flesh. She would have loved to grip him tight. However, he still held her hands captive. Just like his body pinned her in place.

He switched his attention to the other breast, giving it equal teasing play, then switched back again. He seemed determined to torture her.

When he finally released her hands, she could only grab at his hair as he blazed a trail down, his hands divesting her of the scraps of her gown, leaving her naked.

He reared up over her, his eyes glowing with slitted green fire, a true dragon at last. He admired her, stroking a finger down her frame.

Mine. His claim. Hers. It didn't matter. They were joined now. Down he dipped that he might press his lips against her skin, stroking and feathering kisses as he traveled down to her mound.

Her legs were pressed together but immediately parted at his whispered, "Open for me."

She drew her legs up and exposed herself to him, almost arching off the bed at the first lash of his tongue.

He groaned his pleasure as he lapped at her sex. His excitement touched her through their link, and her arousal stroked him right back.

When he finally pushed into her, she was almost past the point of no return. Her sex trembled, hungry for his cock, and he fed it to her, easing his wide shaft into her channel, his body rigid as he tried to hold back.

"Fuck me." She let the dirty words spill past her lips. "Fuck me hard."

It was the secret word that broke his control. He slammed into her, and she screamed, losing her grip on him and, instead, clawing at the sheets as she wrapped her legs around his flanks.

"Again," she cried.

He drew out then pushed back in, hard. Deep. Oh...

Over and over, he slammed into her, each thrust a jolt against her G-spot. Each pump making her channel tighten. Her flesh quiver. Her control waver.

She clawed at him, urging him to go faster, and he listened, even as he manacled her wrists with his hands and drew them over her head once more. He stretched her body and held her as he stroked into her. In. Out. Over and over. Hard, deep slams that had her moaning, and coming.

Oh, yes, she came, her pussy convulsing in orgasmic waves that fisted his shaft. And still, he thrust into her, so big and hard. Although he held her hands prisoner, she could still move somewhat and arched her hips to take him deep, her channel squeezing so tight.

She was going to come again, she could feel it, that building pressure, and this time, she needed him with her.

I need to claim him.

She pulled her hands free and clutched at him, pulling him down to her as he kept thrusting. She kissed him, a hot embrace with plenty of tongue. Her sex clenched around him, and he throbbed inside, pulsing with heat. She rubbed her face against his cheek then along his jaw, marking him with her scent before nuzzling the soft skin of his neck.

There's the spot. Like him, she gave no warning, just clamped down at the moment of climax. He bellowed her name as he came, his hips pushing forward one last time, his seed bathing her womb in heat.

It was done. He'd become her mate.

Welcome to the hoard.

Epilogue

"What do you mean it's not big enough?" Brand eyed the latest house they'd visited, a very decent-sized four bedroom in suburbia with a few acres of land. Not exactly a sprawling ranch in the mountains, mostly because there weren't many of those to begin with and none for sale.

"My hoard needs room, as does yours."

"I am not going to turn into a collector of shit just because I am a dragon." It got easier to say every day. So much had changed since the fateful night when he'd ascended.

First and foremost, *I'm a fucking dragon.* A strange blend of green and gold but not the right kind of green, apparently. His was a new green, and it came with a new power—the power to force a shift.

Very cool, which was why he'd gotten his own family name instead of having to take Aimi's. Apparently, when two dragons mated, the stronger color took precedence. She bore the change rather well—and he truly enjoyed her orally inclined attempts to have him change it to Silvermercgrace. She didn't win. Nor was he adding gold or green to it. Mercer had been good enough for his father, and his father before him, which meant it was good enough for him. Perhaps now that he'd ascended, he could do something about having the Mercer name spoken with more respect.

I might be swamp-born, but at least I've got integrity.

He also had the hottest wife around. He'd mated Aimi Silvergrace. Married her, too, in a lavish ceremony planned by her mother, who grudgingly accepted him—and didn't drop dead when he'd called her Ma and slapped her on the ass.

The entire Silvergrace family welcomed him with open arms—and, in the case of Aunt Matilda, tongue, too. The only thing that marred the celebration of his mating to Aimi was Sue-Ellen. While most of the Mercers came—and some left with precious valuables—his sister hadn't even replied to the invitation Aimi sent.

He'd expected that, but it still hurt. A part of him still couldn't believe she'd turned him away, and so coldly, too. What had happened to the sweet girl he knew?

I know what happened. Uncle Theo. The bastard who was still running around causing havoc. Brandon might have saved Aimi from his machinations, but the man still roamed the world instead of resting six feet under.

Or in our belly. Crunch.

The dark thoughts no longer bothered Brandon, just like he no longer saw a difference between him and his dragon. A part of him sometimes missed his simple gator, but at times, traces of who he used to be still surfaced, like now.

It was hard to miss his swamp roots when he'd turned into something so much grander. Perhaps he only bore a hint of gold, but he'd take it, just like he'd take becoming dragon because it had brought him the greatest gift of all.

Aimi. Love. A hoard to call his own.

A hoard that would get bigger just like Aimi would.

"I heard that," she snapped, but it wasn't said with vehemence, given he cupped her belly. Within his mate's womb, life nestled, his child. His treasure.

And he'd protect both with his life—and crunch the bones of any who thought to touch them.

*

Half a continent away...

She couldn't forget the expression on his face. The betrayal. The hurt. The anger.

I didn't have a choice.

It had almost broken Sue-Ellen's heart to send Brandon away, but telling him the truth, accepting his offer to flee, would have been worse. Uncle Theo had made sure of that. Besides, she couldn't leave *him.* Somehow, someway, there had to be a way to free him. To release him, but until that day came, she'd play along with her uncle's sick plans. Pretend and hurt those who loved her. Hopefully, one day they'd understand.

*

A few days later, a gentleman—AKA human—working for an institute known as Bittech, came home to find Adrianne sprawled on his bed, sifting through his comic book collection.

"Who are you? What are you doing in my apartment?" he demanded, looking adorably flustered behind his glasses.

"I'm the woman who's going to rock your world." Because she did so love a geek.

Especially one with secrets.

The End

Coming next:
Dragon Point 2 - Dragon Squeeze

For more information please see EveLanglais.com

Made in the USA
San Bernardino, CA
03 April 2018